This book belongs to

------------------------------------

# How many Fairy Animals books have you collected?

- Chloe the Kitten
- Bella the Bunny
- Paddy the Puppy
- Mia the Mouse
- Poppy the Pony
- Hailey the Hedgehog

And there are more magical adventures coming very soon!

# Fairy Animals

## of Misty Wood

# Chloe the Kitten

Lily Small

Henry Holt and Company
New York

*With special thanks to Thea Bennett*

Henry Holt and Company, LLC
*Publishers since 1866*
175 Fifth Avenue
New York, New York 10010
mackids.com

First published in the United States in 2015 by
Henry Holt and Company, LLC.
Originally published in Great Britain in 2013 by
Egmont UK Limited.

Library of Congress Cataloging-in-Publication Data
Small, Lily.
Chloe the kitten / Lily Small. — First American edition.
pages cm. — (Fairy animals of Misty Wood ; [1])
"First published in the United States in 2015 by Henry Holt and Company, LLC."
Summary: Chloe, a Cobweb Kitten, is fluttering through Hawthorn Hedgerows
in the enchanted realm of Misty Wood, decorating cobwebs with dewdrops
when she meets a baby mouse who is lost and afraid.
Paper Over Board ISBN 978-1-250-11396-2 — Paperback ISBN 978-1-250-11397-9
[1. Fairies—Fiction. 2. Cats—Fiction. 3. Mice—Fiction.
4. Lost children—Fiction.]
I. Title.
PZ7.S635Chl 2015     [Fic]—dc23     2014026456

Henry Holt books may be purchased for business or promotional use. For information on
bulk purchases, please contact Macmillan Corporate and Premium Sales Department at
(800) 221-7945 x5442 or by e-mail at specialmarkets@macmillan.com.

First American Edition—2015
Printed in the United States of America by R. R. Donnelley &
Sons Company, Harrisonburg, Virginia

Hardcover
1   3   5   7   9   10   8   6   4   2

Paperback
1   3   5   7   9   10   8   6   4   2

# Contents

## CHAPTER ONE

# Good Morning, Misty Wood

It was early morning in Misty Wood. The moon had long since snuggled into his starry bed, and the sun was just beginning to stretch into the sky.

In a cozy cot made of moss and
grass, in a tiny home tucked under
the roots of an old chestnut tree,
a kitten named Chloe was waking
up. She yawned and rubbed the
end of her button nose with a
velvety paw. Then she opened her
eyes and looked at her dandelion
clock.

"Oh no! I'm late!" she cried,
leaping from her bed. But she
stopped short when she caught

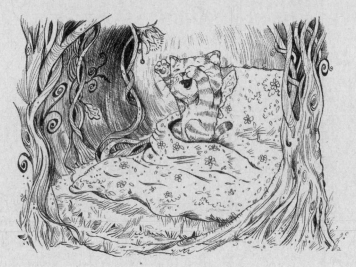

sight of herself in the small pool of water she used as a mirror.

"Puppy tails and poppy seeds!" she meowed. "I can't go out like this!"

3

Chloe's whiskers were flat because she had slept on them. Quickly, she licked her paws and stroked her whiskers until they were shiny and smooth. Then she twisted her head and looked down to check her glittery fairy wings.

You see, Chloe was no ordinary kitten. She was a Cobweb Kitten, one of the many fairy animals who lived in Misty Wood. Every fairy animal in Misty Wood had

a special job to do to make sure it stayed such a beautiful place.

The Bud Bunnies used their twitchy noses to ease flowers into bloom.

The Hedgerow Hedgehogs used their spikes to pick up leaves and keep the ground tidy.

The Holly Hamsters nibbled the holly leaves into shape for Christmas.

And the Cobweb Kittens

5

decorated the cobwebs in the trees with glistening dewdrops so that they sparkled and shone.

Chloe patted her wings into place and smiled down at her reflection.

"Perfect," she purred. "Now I'm ready for work." She picked up her special dewdrop-collecting basket, which had been woven from flower stems.

"No time for breakfast today,"

she said, looking longingly at the acorn cup of milk on her conker table.

The magical spring where the Cobweb Kittens got their dewdrops came to life only while the sun was rising. She had to get there quickly or she would miss it.

Chloe padded over to the door and flung it open. Outside, it was as if Misty Wood was just stirring itself from sleep. A breeze whispered

through the trees, making all the branches sway.

Chloe could hear the first chirps of the birds as they got ready to sing. She opened her wings. They shimmered purple and pink in the first morning light.

"Good morning, Misty Wood!" she said, fluttering up into the air.

Chloe swooped through the trees and out into Bluebell Glade. Down below her she could hear the

tinkle of hundreds of flowery bells as they bobbed in the breeze. She breathed in the bluebells' sweet scent and continued on her way. As she left the glade, she came to Heather Hill.

*It matches my wings*, Chloe thought with a smile as she looked down at the carpet of purple heather.

Next, she did a loop-the-loop over Golden Meadow, hoping to

catch sight of the playful Pollen
Puppies flicking the golden flower
pollen with their tails. But the
cheeky pups were asleep, curled up
on their cushions of moss.

Chloe floated on, enjoying the
sleepy silence. The meadow below
her looked like a rainbow painted
across the land. There were flowers
of every color.

Then she came to Moonshine
Pond. The Moonbeam Moles had

been working hard all night, flying through the sky and dropping moonbeams into the pond to make it look pretty. Now the water had a beautiful pearly glow. It reminded Chloe of the cup of milk in her kitchen, and she suddenly felt very thirsty. She looked at the brightening sky. The sun wasn't quite up yet. As long as she was quick, she should have enough time for a drink.

Chloe flew down and landed on the soft bank of the pond. Putting her basket next to her, she leaned forward to lap the sweet water with her tiny pink tongue. She was careful to be quiet. She didn't want to wake the little moles, who had just gone to bed.

*Mmm*, Chloe thought. *That's better!* The water was delicious. The moonbeams made it taste as sweet as honey. Chloe licked her lips,

unfurled her wings, and fluttered
off again.

At last she came to a beautiful
valley. In the middle of the valley

14

lay a shimmering lake. Silvery mist drifted across the surface of the water. Suddenly, as the first rays of sunlight peeped over the treetops and touched the lake, a jet of water rose high into the air, like a fountain. Fat, glistening dewdrops fell like sparkles from a fairy's wand.

Chloe breathed a sigh of relief. She had arrived at Dewdrop Spring just in time.

The air was filled with excited

15

meowing and purring. There were Cobweb Kittens everywhere! Fluttering their wings as fast as they could, they headed toward the spring, scooping up dewdrops in their special collecting baskets. Every kitten needed to work very hard if all the cobwebs in Misty Wood were to be covered in dewdrops.

"Hello, Chloe," a little tabby kitten called as he flew past.

"Hurry up! You're late!" a white kitten cried, her fairy wings glistening silver and gold.

"Here I come!" Chloe called happily to her friends. "Save some for me!" With a flick of her wings, she dived toward the fountain, ready to collect the dewdrops with her basket. But as she held out her paws, she noticed something terrible.

Her basket was missing!

CHAPTER TWO

## A Helpful Friend

Chloe gave a sad little meow. What
could have happened to her basket?
Then she remembered. She
had set it down on the bank of

Moonshine
Pond when she
stopped for a
drink. She must

have forgotten to pick it up.

"Whiskers and whirlpools!
Whatever am I going to do?" Chloe
cried. She looked anxiously at
the sky.

It was getting lighter and
lighter! There was no time for her to
go all the way back to Moonshine

21

Pond. Soon the sun would be up, and Dewdrop Spring would disappear for another day. Then there would be no dewdrops for her to collect, and she wouldn't be able to decorate her cobwebs.

She watched as, one by one, the other Cobweb Kittens filled their baskets and flew away. Her cobwebs would be the only empty ones in all of Misty Wood!

Chloe flopped down on a patch

of grass and put her fluffy head in her paws. A tear trickled slowly down her nose.

"If I can't decorate my cobwebs, I'll be the worst Cobweb Kitten ever," she sobbed.

"And why can't you decorate your cobwebs?" a cheery voice asked from behind her.

Chloe turned and peeked out from between her paws. A Stardust Squirrel was sitting on a log in

23

front of her, holding an acorn.

Chloe sighed. Normally, she would be pleased to see a Stardust Squirrel.

Stardust Squirrels were some of the most beautiful creatures in Misty Wood. Their soft fur was a glittery gray color, and their wings were a delicate silver and white. When they shook their bushy tails, they sent a shimmer of stardust floating over all the leaves in the

wood, making them glimmer and sparkle.

"I left my basket at Moonshine Pond," Chloe whispered. "Now I can't collect any dewdrops."

"And why did you leave your basket at Moonshine Pond?" the squirrel asked with a twirl of his whiskers.

"Because I'd put it down so I could have a drink," Chloe said, feeling very ashamed.

"I see," said the squirrel. "And why did you need a drink?"

"Because I didn't have any breakfast."

"Oh, you must never leave the house without having breakfast," the squirrel said with a twinkle in his eye. He hopped off the log and bounded over to Chloe, leaving a glittery trail behind him. "I always have a bowl of acorns for breakfast. I was just collecting

26

some, actually." The squirrel held out his acorn to her. "Here, do you want one?"

Chloe shook her head.

The squirrel looked thoughtful for a moment. "What you really need is a walnut," he said.

"No, thank you. I'm much too sad to be hungry," Chloe replied.

The Stardust Squirrel gave a gentle laugh. It sounded like the tinkle of ice crystals on a frozen

lake. "I don't mean to eat," he said. "I mean to make a basket."

Chloe frowned. How could she use a walnut as a basket?

"Wait here," the squirrel said.

Chloe watched as he scampered over to a small tree stump on the bank of the lake, scattering a trail of stardust as he ran. "Ta-da!" he cried, rummaging around in the tree stump. "Just the thing!" He pulled out half a walnut shell.

Chloe looked at the wrinkled shell. "That doesn't look much like a basket," she said sadly.

"Not yet," the squirrel agreed. "But just you watch."

Quick as a flash, the squirrel nibbled two little holes into the side of the shell. Then he picked a thick blade of grass, and with a blur of paws and a flurry of stardust, he tied the grass to the walnut shell to make a sturdy handle.

30

"Oh, I see!" Chloe exclaimed.
"It's a perfect dewdrop-collecting
basket. Thank you!"

"You're welcome," said the squirrel. "Now, are you sure you don't want this tasty acorn?"

Chloe smiled and shook her head. "No, thank you. I've got work to do. Good-bye!" And with that, she flew up into the air and over to the spring.

Flapping her wings hard, Chloe swooped this way and that, catching glistening dewdrops as she flew. The walnut shell was

bigger than her old basket, so she was able to collect more drops than ever before.

Just as Chloe had filled her basket, the sun finished rising above the trees. At once, Dewdrop Spring sank back into the lake.

"Just in time," Chloe said to herself as she fluttered through the valley and off to Hawthorn Hedgerows, the part of Misty Wood she was in charge of decorating.

Hawthorn Hedgerows was right by the edge of the wood. As Chloe flew closer, she spotted the silvery strings of a delicate cobweb clinging to the first hedge. She shivered with excitement. She would soon make it look beautiful.

"I have just the dewdrops for you," Chloe said with a smile as she hovered close to the web. She chose the smallest and sparkliest dewdrops from her basket and

carefully hung them one by one on the threads.

After she had filled the cobweb with dewdrops, she flew back a bit to check her work. The cobweb now sparkled like a jewel! Eagerly, Chloe flew over to the next web and began again. As she worked, she hummed a little tune. She felt so glad to be able to decorate her cobwebs after all.

Chloe was starting her fifth

cobweb when she felt a gentle

tap on the top of her head. She

looked up and saw a spider

dangling above her on a strand of silky web.

"Sorry to trouble you," the spider said, pointing a spindly leg toward the part of the hedge Chloe had just finished. "But I was wondering why you haven't decorated my web."

"I have!" Chloe answered in surprise. "Look, I'll show you." She spread her wings and flew back along the hedge. But to her dismay,

37

she saw that the spider was right.
His cobweb was empty! There
were no dewdrops on it at all.
And all the other cobwebs Chloe
had spent so long decorating
were bare, too. Her dewdrops had
completely disappeared!

## CHAPTER THREE

# The Dewdrop Thief

Chloe flew this way and that, searching for the dewdrops. They were nowhere to be seen.

"I told you," the spider said,

while solemnly blinking his tiny
eyes.

"But I just don't understand!"
Chloe meowed. "I'm sure I did that
hedgerow. Look, it was the same as
this one."

Chloe turned to show the spider
the hedge she had just begun to
decorate with sparkly dewdrops.
But much to her surprise, they were
gone, too!

"Someone must have stolen

40

them!" Chloe cried. She gulped.

*Someone . . . or something.*

"You mean we have a dewdrop thief?" the spider asked, frowning.

Chloe nodded. "I'm afraid so."

"I don't like the sound of that," said the spider, and he scurried off as fast as his eight legs would carry him.

Chloe slumped down to the ground. "Whatever will I tell the other fairy animals?" she sighed. "They will think I haven't done any work at all this morning."

She gazed gloomily into her basket. There were lots of lovely,

plump dewdrops left, but if she
hung them up, would they just
disappear, too?

Then Chloe had a brilliant idea.
"Cockleshells and conkers!" she
cried with a grin. "I know what I
will do."

Carefully, she lifted out a
shimmering dewdrop from her
basket. She placed it gently on a
silky strand of the nearest cobweb.
Then Chloe added two more

43

dewdrops so that all three hung in a row, sparkling like precious jewels.

"Ah, well," Chloe declared loudly. "I think it's time that I went and had some breakfast." She gave her tummy a pat. "Ooh, I'm so hungry."

Chloe unfurled her wings and started to fly away. But instead of leaving Hawthorn Hedgerows, she swerved around the back of a large oak tree. Behind its huge trunk, Chloe was well hidden, but if she peeked out, she had a perfect view of the cobweb she had just decorated.

"Now all I have to do is wait," she said to herself, "and see if the dewdrop thief comes back."

45

Chloe waited. And as she waited, she began to wonder if her idea had been such a good one after all.

*What if the dewdrop thief is very big?* she thought.

46

The branches of the old oak tree creaked.

*What if the dewdrop thief is scary?*

A breeze shivered through the leaves.

*What if the dewdrop thief doesn't like Cobweb Kittens?*

There was a rustling in the hedgerow. Chloe peered around the tree. The thread of the silvery web was trembling and the dewdrops were quivering. Was the thief coming?

Chloe crouched down in her hiding place, not daring to look. The rustling stopped, and there was silence.

Gathering up all her courage, Chloe peeked out. What she saw wasn't big. And it wasn't scary. There, in the middle of the clearing, was a tiny Moss Mouse.

Moss Mice were another type of fairy animal. Their special job was to shape Misty Wood's moss

into velvety cushions for the other
animals to sleep on. But this timid
creature looked much too small
for any kind of job. He was just a
baby!

For a moment, the mouse sat all alone in the middle of the clearing. Then he tiptoed over to the hedge. With a flutter of his tiny wings, he flew up to the cobweb and began lapping thirstily at the nearest dewdrop.

Chloe stared in disbelief. To think that she had been scared of a terrible thief when all this time her hard work was being slurped up by a greedy mouse!

"What are you doing?" she cried, flying out from her hiding place.

The little Moss Mouse was so startled he fell backward from the web, did a somersault, and landed with a *plop* on a toadstool below. The dewdrops splashed down on top of him like rain.

"Those dewdrops are not for drinking. They're to make the hedges look pretty," Chloe

51

went on. "I spent ages hanging them."

But as she hovered above the Moss Mouse, Chloe saw that the water running down his pointy nose wasn't from the dewdrops. Big, splashy tears were spilling from his eyes and soaking his downy cheeks.

"I'm sorry," the little mouse said in a trembly voice. "But I was very thirsty, and I didn't know where

else to get a drink." He put his head in his tiny paws and sobbed some more.

Chloe felt awful. He was such a young mouse, and he looked so sad. She shouldn't have been cross with him.

"It's all right," Chloe purred, patting his back with her paw. "I'm sorry I shouted at you. What's your name, and why are you so thirsty?"

"My name is Morris," the mouse sniffed. "I'm thirsty because I . . . I . . ." He started to cry again. "I lost my mommy and daddy."

"You *lost* them?" Chloe asked.

Morris nodded sadly.

"How did you lose them?"

Morris looked down. "We were going to visit Grandma," he whispered, "and I flew off to look at some buttercups. And then . . . and then . . . well, I couldn't find

my way back." He let out another tiny sob.

Chloe picked a velvety leaf from the hedge next to them and handed it to him. "Here," she said. "Wipe your eyes."

Morris dabbed at his face with the leaf.

"When did you lose your mommy and daddy?" Chloe asked.

"Yesterday morning," Morris replied.

55

"Yesterday morning?" Chloe stared at him. "No wonder you're thirsty."

"I was only going to drink one dewdrop," Morris whimpered, "but they were so tasty. I'm sorry." He hung his tiny head again.

Chloe thought of how the Stardust Squirrel had helped her when she'd lost her basket. Now it was her turn to help.

"Don't worry," she said with

57

a smile. "I'll help you find your mommy and daddy—I promise. Do you have any idea where your home is?"

Morris nodded. "It's by the lions."

Chloe stared at him in shock. "By the *lions*?"

"Yes," the little mouse replied. "By the big lions."

Chloe gulped. She didn't know there were lions in Misty Wood.

58

Her heart began to pound. Finding Morris's home might be a lot scarier than she had thought!

CHAPTER FOUR

# The Rainbow Slide

Morris looked up at Chloe. His
shiny black eyes blinked at her
anxiously.

"Please will you take me home?"

he squeaked. "I miss my mommy and daddy."

Chloe's tummy gave a little lurch. She had to keep her promise. It was up to her to get Morris back safely, however scary it might be.

"Ladybugs and lollipops!" she whispered to herself. "If this little mouse is brave enough to live next door to some big lions, then as sure as my wings are purple, I am brave enough to take him there."

She turned to Morris again. "Is your home very far away?"

"Oh yes. Miles and miles," Morris replied.

"In that case," Chloe said, "I think it would be better if I carried you. Your wings are so small, and you must be very tired. You can climb onto my back. We'll fly above Misty Wood together. You can help me look out for the lions."

Morris clapped his tiny paws.

"Thank you! Thank you!" he squeaked excitedly.

Chloe tucked her basket of dewdrops beneath a hedge to keep it safe. Then she crouched down low as Morris clambered onto her back and perched between her wings.

"Hold on tight!" Chloe called. With a flick of her shimmering wings she flew up into the sky, brushing the treetops with her sparkly tail as she rose higher and higher.

63

"Wheeeeeeeee!" Morris cried.

Far below, Misty Wood lay stretched out like a colorful patchwork quilt, glimmering in the early morning sunshine. Somewhere down there, among the meadows and the mountains, the grasslands and the glades, Morris's family was waiting anxiously for him. But where were they?

A flash of golden fur across

a patch of brilliant blue caught Chloe's eye.

Lions? Chloe caught her breath and looked closer.

No, it was only the Pollen Puppies. They were awake and playing in Bluebell Glade, flicking the pollen here and there with their tails so that even more flowers would grow.

*I wonder if they know where the lions live*, Chloe thought. She

called over her shoulder to her tiny passenger. "Hold on, Morris! We're going down!"

With a flutter of fairy wings, Chloe landed in the glade.

"Hey! What's going on?" Petey, a floppy-eared puppy, cried as he bounced over.

"Have you come to play with us?" his friend Max asked as he scampered up. Clouds of yellow pollen fell like gold dust from

68

his coat. "Look, everyone! It's a Cobweb Kitten who wants to be a Pollen Puppy."

"No, I don't wa—" Chloe began, but Max was already running around her, his tail wagging.

"First of all, you have to learn how to bark," Max said. "Show her how to bark, Petey."

"But I don't—" Chloe spluttered. Before she could say any more, Petey started barking.

"And wag your tail," Max called. "You have to wag your tail if you want to be a Pollen Puppy. It's what we do best."

Petey barked even louder, and other puppies started joining in,

too, until the whole glade became a
blur of wagging tails and barking
puppies.

"But—" said Chloe.

"Oh dear," squeaked Morris.

"*I don't want to bark and I don't want to wag my tail and I don't want to be a Pollen Puppy!*" Chloe shouted at the top of her voice.

The glade fell silent.

"Oh," said Petey.

"No need to shout," sniffed Max.

"I'm sorry," said Chloe. "I'm sure it's great fun being a Pollen Puppy, but something very sad has happened, and I need your help."

72

"Well, why didn't you say so?" said Max.

"What's happened?" asked Petey.

"When I was hanging up my dewdrops this morning, I found this little mouse." Chloe gestured with her paw.

The puppies, who hadn't noticed Morris because he was so small, gathered closer.

"His name is Morris and he got

73

lost on the way to his grandma's, so I'm helping him find his way back home. But"—Chloe gulped and dropped her voice to a whisper— "Morris says he lives near some lions! Do you know if there are any lions living here in Misty Wood?"

"Lions?" A spotted puppy called Freckles started to laugh. "Has anyone seen any lions?"

"Grrr!" Max bared his tiny white teeth.

"Growl!" Petey sharpened his pointy claws.

"Roar!" Freckles shook his head so the pollen floated around his ears like a golden mane. "Lions, you say? Here we are!"

Chloe shook her head crossly. Usually the cheeky Pollen Puppies made her laugh, but this was no time for joking. She had to get Morris home.

"Please can you help me?" she begged. "Morris has been lost for a very long time."

At the sound of Chloe's sad voice, the puppies stopped their teasing.

"Sorry," said Max. "We were only joking."

76

"We really don't know where the lions live," Petey piped up.

"Hmm," said Freckles. "Why don't you try looking in Crystal Cave at the side of Heather Hill?"

"Crystal Cave? That's a great idea!" Chloe cried.

"You know how to get there, don't you?" said Max. "Just follow the rainbow."

"Thank you, puppies," Chloe said with a smile. "Hold on tight,

Morris. We're going up again!"

"Good-bye! Good luck!" the Pollen Puppies called, their furry tails waving wildly.

"And if you do ever want to be a Pollen Puppy, just let us know," Max called out.

Crystal Cave was tucked away on the very darkest side of Heather Hill. Chloe knew exactly where to go.

Usually the sight of her favorite

hill, covered with pretty purple flowers, made her feel happy. Today, however, she felt scared. She had never seen a lion before, but she knew they were the biggest members of the cat family. *And a Cobweb Kitten is the smallest,* she thought nervously.

Now someone even smaller needed her help. Morris was counting on her to find his parents. She couldn't let him down.

79

Suddenly, there was a tiny shout in her left ear. "Look, Chloe!" Morris cried. "A rainbow! A rainbow!"

Sure enough, a rainbow of sparkling light arched across the sky in front of them. Chloe flapped her glittery wings with all her might until she landed on the very top of the rainbow.

"Hold tight, Morris! We're going for a ride!" she called over her shoulder.

80

"Wheeeeeeeee!" Morris squealed as they started to slide down the rainbow.

Faster and faster they slid. Chloe's whiskers tingled as the air whistled through them. Finally, they landed with a soft bump on the far side of Heather Hill, right at the mouth of Crystal Cave.

The warm colors of the crystals in the cave shimmered across Chloe's fur like fairy lights. For a

81

moment, she almost forgot what she was looking for. The rainbow ride had been so much fun and Crystal Cave was so pretty—it couldn't possibly be home to anything scary. Could it?

Suddenly, a very deep voice boomed out from the depths of the cave. "Who's there?"

Chloe fell back in fright.

"What do you want?" the voice rang out again.

83

Chloe crouched down. She was terrified.

On her back, Morris gave a small squeal and cowered into her trembling fur.

A dark shadow loomed out of the cave. Chloe could hardly bear to look. Were the Pollen Puppies right? Could this be the hiding place of a large and scary lion?

84

CHAPTER FIVE

# Crystal Cave

"Well?" the voice boomed again. "I said, who's there?"

Chloe blinked against the dazzling light. "Oh!" she cried. "You're—"

"I'm what?" the figure boomed.

"You're not a lion!"

"Of course I'm not a lion!"

Chloe laughed with relief as the figure emerged. Now that he was standing in the sunlight, she could see he wasn't anything like a lion. He was a Bark Badger. From his broad black-and-white shoulders sprouted a pair of delicate, graying wings. The stocky creature shuffled forward and frowned down at them.

"Well," he said, "what do you little 'uns want? Apart from telling me that I'm not a lion!"

Chloe opened her mouth, but no sound came out. She might not have been face-to-face with a lion, but she *was* still a little scared.

Bark Badgers were very kind fairy animals, but they were also very big and strong. Their nimble paws carved the most beautiful patterns into the tree barks of Misty

87

Wood, and they took their job very seriously indeed. Unlike the cheeky Pollen Puppies, they had no time for jokes or tricks.

Gathering all her courage, Chloe raised her head and began to speak. "I'm helping this little Moss Mouse," she said with a trembling voice. "He's lost and I'm trying to find his home. He says it's near the lions, but I have no idea where the lions live. The

Pollen Puppies suggested I try looking here."

"Hmm." The Bark Badger stroked his whiskery chin thoughtfully. "Lions, you say?"

89

Chloe nodded.

"I have lived in Misty Wood forever and a day, and I have never known there to be lions here," the Bark Badger said.

"Oh, bother and broomsticks," Chloe said with a sad little sigh. "Will I ever get Morris home?"

The Bark Badger's wise black eyes began to twinkle. "I can see you are a very helpful and caring kitten," he said. "So I will give you

some advice. Are you listening

carefully?"

Chloe leaned forward. "Oh

yes," she said eagerly.

"There is a place in Misty Wood

that is very dark and very quiet,"

the Bark Badger whispered in her

ear. "No birds sing. No squirrels

scamper. Everything is silent and

still. It is in the Heart of Misty

Wood, and few have ever been

there." He tapped the side of his

nose knowingly with a long, pointy claw. "If there are lions in Misty Wood, that is where they will be hiding."

Chloe gave a small meow of fear. "Really, truly?" she whispered.

"Really, truly." The Bark Badger nodded.

"Oh. Well. Thank you," Chloe squeaked, trying to look braver than she felt. Her mind was racing. She had never ventured into the

Heart of Misty Wood before. It sounded very dark. And very scary.

"What did he say? What did he say?" Morris squeaked from her back.

"He said we are close to finding your home," Chloe replied. She couldn't let Morris know how nervous she was.

"Yippee! Yippee!" Morris cried, and did a little somersault behind Chloe's ear.

"Well, we'd better be off, then." Chloe smiled bravely at the Bark Badger. "Here I go. Into the Heart of Misty Wood." She paused. "Into the darkness," she went on, her voice wobbling ever so slightly.

"Perhaps you would like something to light your way?" the Bark Badger suggested.

Chloe smiled. "Oh yes, please."

The Bark Badger shuffled back into his cave and soon returned

94

with a piece of crystal taken from the roof of the cave. It glowed with so many different colors it was as if he were holding a piece of rainbow.

"Thank you. It's very beautiful," Chloe breathed.

"You're welcome," the badger replied. "Now, hold it carefully ahead of you and let the light show you the way. Good-bye." The Bark Badger waved a large paw at them. "And good luck!"

Chloe flew up into the air, clutching the crystal tightly in her front paws. "Good-bye, Mr. Bark

Badger!" she called. "And thank you again!"

Soon they had left the beauty of Crystal Cave far behind and were venturing deeper into Misty Wood. Chloe held the rainbow crystal before her. Its warm glow lit up the gloom but also cast shadows that darted among the tree trunks. Sometimes it looked as if strange shapes were following them as they flew.

"It's so dark," Morris squeaked. "And scary, too."

"It's only the light playing tricks on us," Chloe said, trying to sound cheerful. "Now, Morris, do you recognize anything?"

"No," Morris replied sadly.

Chloe flew even deeper into the tangle of trees. It was very dark. And very quiet.

Up ahead, she saw two pinpoints of light coming from

the trunk of a tree. Then they disappeared. Then they beamed brightly at her once more. On and off, on and off the lights blinked.

Chloe's tummy gave a fearful lurch as she realized what she was looking at. They weren't lights.

They were eyes blinking at her from the dark.

CHAPTER SIX

# A Magical Wish

Chloe meowed in surprise and
fluttered onto the solid branch of an
oak tree with a tiny thud.

"Ouch," Morris squeaked.

"Sshhhh," Chloe whispered, hardly daring to breathe. Up above her, the eyes blinked again. Chloe gulped. Had she found the lions at last?

The leaves on the tree above her started to rustle, and from the darkness came a soft noise. It sounded a bit like a lion, stretching its paws and shaking out its mane.

Chloe shrank back in fear as the leaves slowly parted to reveal

the eyes again, growing bigger and
bigger.

But, to Chloe's relief, there was
no lion's mane to be seen. Instead,
the eyes were framed by the
feathery face of an owl. A scarlet
beak chirped a welcome.

"T'wit, t'woo! Who are
*you*?"

Chloe gave a little sigh of
delight. "Magic and milk shakes,"
she whispered softly to herself.

"Are you . . . are you . . . the Wise Wishing Owl?"

The owl nodded three times.

Morris squeaked and Chloe

trembled with excitement. Never
in her wildest dreams had she
imagined she would come nose-to-
beak with the most magical animal
in all of Misty Wood.

The Wise Wishing Owl, with
her scarlet beak and feathers of
gold, was the cleverest and oldest
creature in the wood—as old as the
oldest oak trees. She had the power
to make wishes come true . . . if you
were able to find her.

"You are very far from home, little Cobweb Kitten. Are you lost?" The Wise Wishing Owl's voice was like the most beautiful piece of music Chloe had ever heard.

"Yes," Chloe said. "I'm trying to help this little Moss Mouse, Morris, find his family. I've been searching and searching, but I can't find them anywhere!" A silvery tear ran down Chloe's cheek, and she sniffed sadly.

106

"There, there, little kitten. Don't cry," the Wise Wishing Owl said. "You found me, and not many do. Now, do you have any idea where Morris might live?"

"Yes. He says he lives by the lions," Chloe answered with a gulp.

"The lions! The lions!" Morris squeaked.

"Oh." The Wise Wishing Owl furrowed her feathery brow. "I have lived in Misty Wood for a very,

very long time, but I have never heard of any lions living here."

Chloe gave a long, sad sigh. "That's what everyone says."

The Wise Wishing Owl turned her head slowly from side to side three times. "It helps me to think," she explained when she saw Chloe staring at her. "And now that I have thought, I believe I know where Morris lives."

"Hurray!" Morris squeaked.

"You do?" Chloe's face lit up with excitement. "Is it very far?"

"It certainly is," the Wise Wishing Owl said with a nod. "Perhaps I could have a word with young Morris?"

Chloe tilted her head.

"Hello, Morris," said the Wise Wishing Owl.

"Hello," Morris squeaked. "I've lost my mommy and daddy."

"I understand," said the Wise

Wishing Owl gently. "Now, let me ask you something. What is your dearest wish?"

"To find my mommy and daddy," Morris said with a little sigh.

"Then I shall grant your wish," the Wise Wishing Owl said solemnly.

"Hurray!" Morris cheered.

"Really?" Chloe asked.

"Of course," the Wise Wishing Owl replied. "I always help a fairy animal in need. You have done your best, Chloe, and I can see

you are very brave. But you also look very tired. Why not leave the rest to me?"

"Oh yes, please," Chloe said.

"Then hold on to your whiskers!" the Wise Wishing Owl hooted. "I'm sending you home." The owl flapped her huge wings up and down three times.

A gentle breeze began to play around the tree branch. Chloe felt a twig brush her face, and the breeze

grew stronger. Suddenly, she and Morris were lifted skyward. Up and up they spiraled, traveling faster with each twist and turn. Misty Wood spun beneath them, a blur of colors and light.

Chloe laughed excitedly. It was even better than sliding down the rainbow!

All of a sudden the spinning stopped, and they landed with a bump on the ground, a cloud of

yellow cushioning their fall.

"Lions!" Chloe gasped, her
head still dizzy. But as her eyes
adjusted to the bright daylight, she
saw they hadn't landed on the back
of a fierce yellow lion, but in a field
of golden dandelions.

"Lions! Lions!" Morris cried in
delight.

"Sunshine and sparkles!" Chloe
said with a smile. "Look! We're
in Dandelion Dell!" She stretched

115

out on the blanket of bobbing yellow flowers. "So you live by the *dande*lions, Morris."

"Yes! Yes!" Morris scampered down from her back and did a cartwheel in delight.

Chloe chuckled. "I should have known there wouldn't be any actual lions in Misty Wood."

Just then, there was a rustling sound in the dell. The dandelions started to sway. Something—or

someone—was making its way toward them. Chloe heard a small, high-pitched noise grow louder as it got nearer.

"Morris, Morris, Morris, MORRIS!"

Across the yellow field, a procession of Moss Mice appeared, marching through the dandelions.

"Mommy! Daddy!" Morris cried, and scampered into the arms

of two very relieved-looking Moss Mice. The rest of the procession cheered and waved.

Morris turned to Chloe. "My mommy and daddy! We found them!"

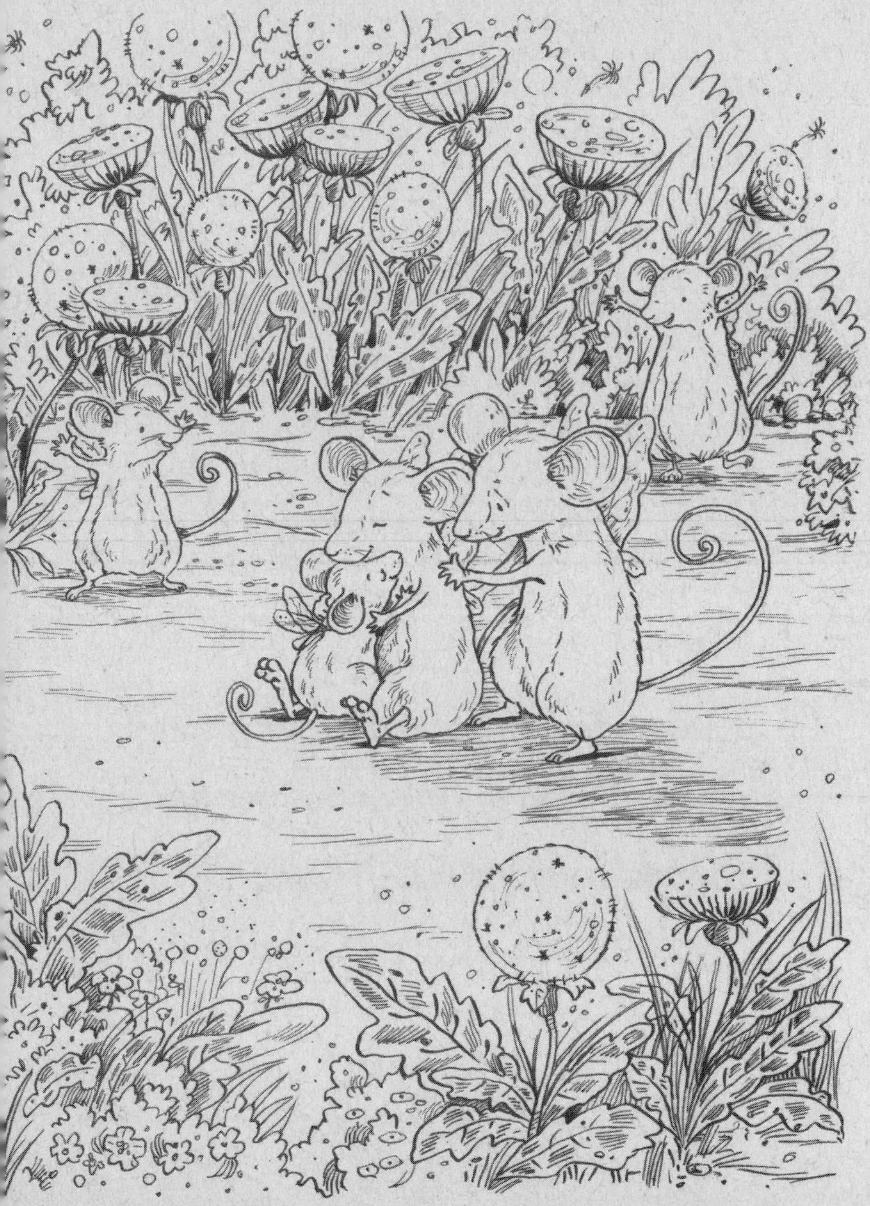

CHAPTER SEVEN

# Home at Last!

As the Moss Mice gathered around, Chloe told them all about her and Morris's adventures.

"You thought we lived by some

scary lions?" Morris's mommy said, her eyes wide.

Chloe nodded.

"And yet you still tried to find us?" Morris's daddy asked.

Chloe nodded again.

"Well then, you are a very brave Cobweb Kitten," he said, and all the other Moss Mice started clapping and cheering in agreement.

Morris wriggled out of his

mommy's arms and scampered back up onto Chloe's back. "Thank you for helping me, Chloe," he whispered in her ear. "I'll never forget you."

Chloe fizzed with happiness to the very tips of her whiskers.

Morris's daddy clapped his paws. "Tell us, Chloe, is there any way we can repay you? We Moss Mice may be small, but we are very hard workers. If there is

anything you need, just let us know."

"Anything at all," Morris's mommy added.

Chloe scratched her head. "Thank you, but I can't think of anything I need, now that Morris is safe. I suppose I'd better get back to—" Chloe gasped. "Decorations and dandelions! My cobwebs!"

She looked at the sun, now high in the sky. It seemed very long ago

123

that she had woken with the sunrise

and set off to get her dewdrops.

"Yes, yes, there is something you

can help me with," she said eagerly.

Chloe had never flown with so
many other fairy animals before.
The Moss Mice spun and tumbled
through the sky like dandelion
seeds scattering on the breeze.

"Here we are!" Chloe cried
at last, spotting the Hawthorn
Hedgerows far below them.

In a swirl of excitement, the
Moss Mice floated down to land in
the clearing.

Chloe's basket of dewdrops was
still where she had left it, tucked
under one of the hedges. After

Chloe showed them what to do,
the Moss Mice set to work,
singing happy songs as they
scampered about. Soon, all
the cobwebs were decorated
with sparkling dewdrops, and
Hawthorn Hedgerows had never
looked so beautiful.

Chloe clapped with glee.

"Thank you!" she cried.

"Don't mention it," said Morris's daddy. "Now, after so much excitement, I think we all deserve a treat."

"Treat! Treat!" Morris cried.

"We shall have a picnic," Morris's daddy declared, and all the other mice started to cheer. "And, Chloe, you must be our very special guest."

Chloe was so happy she thought

she might burst. What a magical day it had been! She might not have found any lions, but she had certainly found plenty of new friends.

It was lovely living in Misty Wood.

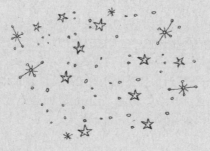

# Misty Wood Quiz

## Misty Wood is home to all sorts of fairy animals. Which Fairy Animal would you be if you lived there? Take this fun quiz to find out.

**1** Misty Wood is full of beautiful things. Which of these do you think is the prettiest?

A) sparkly dewdrops
B) velvety green moss
C) a brightly colored flower
D) a floaty cloud of pollen

**2** Each fairy animal is cute and special in its own way. If you were a fairy animal, which of these would you most like to have?

A) silky fur
B) silver whiskers
C) soft, floppy ears
D) a fluffy, waggy tail

**3** Of all the lovely places in Misty Wood, which is your favorite?

   A) Dewdrop Spring
   B) Dandelion Dell
   C) Bluebell Glade
   D) Honeydew Meadow

**4** The fairy animals stay cozy and warm at night. If you were a fairy animal, where would you like to sleep?

   A) on a cozy cot of moss and soft grass
   B) in a snuggly bed under an oak tree
   C) in a lovely warm warren beneath a cluster of mulberry bushes
   D) in a sweet little den under a hawthorn hedge

**5** Each fairy animal has a favorite thing to do in Misty Wood. What do you like doing the most?

   A) decorating things and making everything around you look pretty
   B) using your imagination to make things
   C) playing with beautiful flowers
   D) running, jumping, telling jokes, and playing games

## Mostly A

You would be a Cobweb Kitten! Cobweb Kittens love pretty things, especially the glittery dewdrops they use to decorate the Misty Wood cobwebs. They enjoy collecting things in their baskets and drinking milk.

## Mostly B

You would be a Moss Mouse! Moss Mice can be quite shy and quiet. They love stories and cuddling on their soft green cushions.

## Mostly C

You would be a Bud Bunny! Bud Bunnies have cute, floppy ears and soft pink noses. They love playing in the sunshine with their friends, especially among the flowers.

## Mostly D

You would be a Pollen Puppy! Pollen Puppies have loads of energy and like to run. They also love having fun and making other fairy animals laugh.

# Misty Wood Treasure Hunt

Misty Wood is full of treasures, from the moonbeams in Moonshine Pond to a cave made of crystal and a rainbow to slide down. Try to find these treasures in your park or garden:

A lovely green leaf

A bright yellow dandelion

A pretty feather

A piece of velvety moss

A prickly pinecone

A snow-white daisy

# Misty Wood Wishes

*"T'wit, t'woo! I am the Wise Wishing Owl. I live in the Heart of Misty Wood. Not many people find me, but those who do may ask me to grant them their wishes."*

If you could have three wishes granted by the Wise Wishing Owl, what would they be? You can write them below.

*A wish for my best friend:*

_____

_____

*A wish for my mom or dad:*

_____

_____

*A wish just for me:*

_____

_____

# Fairy Animals

## of Misty Wood

## Bella the Bunny

Lily Small

Henry Holt and Company
New York

*With special thanks to Thea Bennett*

Henry Holt and Company, LLC
*Publishers since 1866*
175 Fifth Avenue
New York, New York 10010
mackids.com

First published in the United States in 2015
by Henry Holt and Company, LLC.
Originally published in Great Britain in 2013
by Egmont UK Limited.

Library of Congress Cataloging-in-Publication Data
Small, Lily.
Bella the bunny / Lily Small. — First American edition.
pages cm. — (Fairy animals of Misty Wood ; [2])
Summary: Bella, a fairy rabbit, helps Lexi the ladybug understand that if she does her
best she will be judged on what she accomplishes, rather than on her appearance.
Paper Over Board ISBN 978-1-250-11396-2 — Paperback ISBN 978-1-250-11397-9
[1. Fairies—Fiction. 2. Rabbits—Fiction. 3. Ladybugs—Fiction.
4. Self-confidence—Fiction.] I. Title.
PZ7.S635Bel 2015          [Fic]—dc23          2014039993

Henry Holt books may be purchased for business or promotional use. For information on
bulk purchases, please contact the Macmillan Corporate and Premium Sales Department
at (800) 221-7945 x5442 or by e-mail at specialmarkets@macmillan.com.

First American Edition—2015
Printed in the United States of America by R. R. Donnelley &
Sons Company, Harrisonburg, Virginia

Hardcover
1  3  5  7  9  10  8  6  4  2

Paperback
1  3  5  7  9  10  8  6  4  2

# Contents

CHAPTER ONE

# The Talking Bud

Spring had come to Misty Wood.
The early morning sun could see
lots of baby plants starting to grow
on the ground below as he rose

through the bright blue sky. With a warm smile, the sun reached out his beams to help the plants push through the soil.

High among the trees, there was a flash of silver. It was a little bunny! She had soft silver-gray fur, violet eyes that sparkled like jewels ... and a pair of golden fairy wings. Her name was Bella, and she was a Bud Bunny—one of the fairy animals who lived in Misty Wood.

As she flitted through the trees, she sang a song about the special job she was going to do—open the beautiful spring flowers.

*Shine on, shine on, big, bright sun!*

*I'm on my way to have some fun.*

*I'll be spending happy hours*

*Turning buds into flowers!*

Suddenly, Bella felt something trickle down her fur. Droplets of rain had started to fall. *Pitter-patter* went the raindrops as they bounced on

4

the leaves. Bella smiled as the water tickled her nose. She liked the rain just as much as she liked the sun—it helped the flowers to grow, too!

Bella twitched her velvety nose. The leaves and the earth and the new plants smelled lovely in the rain. Everything was green and fresh.

*Misty Wood will be even more beautiful when I've done my job!* Bella thought. She twirled her wings and did a happy somersault. *Soon*

*there'll be lovely flowers everywhere!*

Just as quickly as it had begun, the rain stopped and the sun was shining again.

"No time to lose," Bella told herself. "I must hurry to Bluebell Glade. There are hundreds of bluebells there, just waiting for me to open them."

She darted off through the trees, singing more of her song.

*Little buds just wait for me.*

*I'll come soon to help you be*

*Pretty flowers fresh and bright,*

*Blue and yellow, pink and white.*

"Hello, Bella!"

Bella spun around at the sound

of her name. Carla, a Cobweb

Kitten, was flying along behind

her. Her wings sparkled in the

sunlight as she hurried to catch up.

Carla was Bella's best friend.

She had white fur the same color

as the mist that gathered under

7

the trees—and beautiful spots that
looked like chocolate chips.

Carla flew up, and the two
friends touched noses to say hello.

"I can't stop. I must get to
Bluebell Glade," Bella explained.
Then she noticed the little basket

Carla was carrying, made from tightly woven flower stems. "Your basket looks heavy today, Carla."

"It's full to the brim with dewdrops," Carla replied proudly.

Just like the Bud Bunnies, the Cobweb Kittens had an important job to do in Misty Wood. Every day, the Cobweb Kittens gathered dewdrops and hung them on cobwebs so they glittered in the sunlight.

Suddenly, Bella's ears quivered. She could hear a buzzing noise.

*Bzzzzzzzz. Bzzzzzzzzzzz.*

"What's that?" Bella said, spinning around.

"Look!" Carla cried.

Bella turned to see what Carla had spotted. A cloud of tiny wings glinted in the sunshine. Hundreds of insects were flying toward them.

A small blue June bug bumped into Bella's nose.

"Oops, sorry!" the June bug squeaked before whizzing on.

Then a swarm of striped hoverflies buzzed by.

"Hey, where are you going?" called Carla.

"*Zzzzz*. Musssst dassshhhh!" the hoverflies replied, following the June bug.

"I've never seen so many insects," Bella told Carla. "I wonder what's going on."

A big yellow butterfly fluttered up to them.

"Hello, Mr. Butterfly," Bella said. "Where are you all going?"

"Today is the Misty Wood Insect Sports Day," he said. "I'm the chief steward!" He twirled his long antennae grandly.

"Wow!" Bella gasped.

"Insect Sports Day! How could we have forgotten?" said Carla. "It happens every year on Heather Hill."

12

"Do come along. Everyone's welcome," the friendly butterfly

13

said before whooshing after the hoverflies.

"Oh, I wish we could go," Carla sighed. "Watching the insects race must be so much fun!"

"I know!" said Bella. "Maybe we can, if we're really quick with our cobwebs and flower buds."

"Great idea!" Carla exclaimed. "I'd better start hanging up these dewdrops, then. Bye, Bella. See you later at Heather Hill." Carla

rubbed noses with her friend and
flew off toward the edge of the
wood, where the cobwebs were
waiting for their dewdrops.

"Bye!" Bella called after her.
Then she set off toward Bluebell
Glade, humming her happy song.

When Bella reached the glade,
she swooped down and landed
among the bluebells. Each one had
lots of tight green buds just waiting
to be opened. Bella's nose tingled

with excitement. When she finished
her work, the glade would be a
sea of blue, and the sweet smell of
the flowers would drift all through
Misty Wood.

She hopped over to a bluebell
stem and twitched her nose against
the biggest bud. Very slowly, the
petals began to unfurl. Bella hopped
back and watched, her whiskers
quivering in delight. This was her
favorite part of her job. It was

like watching a beautiful present unwrap itself. She held her breath, and a pretty blue flower, the same shape as a fairy's cap, burst out.

Bella sang happily as she hopped and bounced her way over to another bud.

*A hippity-hop and a hoppity-hip.*

*Opening flowers makes me skip!*

Soon she had opened dozens of bluebells. They tinkled like bells in the breeze, and the glade

17

was filled with their sweet scent.

Then there was just one flower left to open. Bella hopped over to it eagerly. One more flower and then she could go to Insect Sports Day! But just as she placed her velvety nose next to the bud, something very strange happened.

"Please don't!" a voice squeaked.

Bella hopped back on her heels and stared at the plant in shock. The voice was coming from the

flower! In all the time she'd been a
Bud Bunny, Bella had never heard
a bud speak to her before. What
was going on?

CHAPTER TWO

# A Sad Ladybug

Bella pricked up her ears and listened. Everything was quiet. Maybe she'd imagined the voice. "After all, buds can't talk,

20

or can they?" she said to herself.

She hopped up close to the bluebell again. She was about to touch her nose to the bud when—

"Didn't you hear what I said?" the bud squeaked. "Please, please leave me alone!"

Bella jumped back in surprise. She definitely hadn't imagined the voice this time.

"Don't open me," the flower pleaded. Its voice was quivery

now—as if it was about to cry.

"Why ever not?" Bella asked.

The bud went quiet again.

Bella leaned in close. "Don't you want to be a pretty flower?" she whispered.

The bud made a noise that sounded like a sigh. Then it said, in a teeny-tiny voice, "Well . . . the thing is . . ."

"I can't hear you," Bella said.

The voice spoke again, a bit

louder now. "The thing is . . . you see . . . I like being a bud. I don't want to change."

Bella's ears shot up and her eyes opened wide. She couldn't believe what the flower was saying. "Don't be silly!" she said. "You'll be a beautiful bluebell!"

"No!" squeaked the bud.

But Bella's nose was already twitching. The bud was probably just shy. Once Bella had opened

23

it, and the flower saw how lovely it looked, it would soon change its mind. She pressed her nose against the bud and wiggled it.

One by one, the shiny blue petals unpeeled to reveal the biggest, brightest bluebell in the whole glade.

"There, see. You're beautiful!" Bella cried, clapping her silky paws.

"No!" the voice wailed. "I'm not beautiful at all. Look at me!"

24

Something flew out of the
flower, zoomed toward Bella, and
landed on her nose. Bella squinted
to see what was there.

It was a tiny ladybug! She had
a tiny frown on her face.

"Why didn't you listen to me?" the ladybug whispered. "Why couldn't you leave me in there?"

"I'm really sorry." Bella's ears flopped down over her face, the way they always did when she felt upset. "I . . . I thought it was the flower talking."

"But flowers don't talk!" the ladybug exclaimed.

"I know, but . . ." Now Bella frowned. "What were you doing

26

hiding inside a bluebell bud?" she asked.

The ladybug looked sad. "I was hiding from Insect Sports Day."

"What? But why?" Bella asked. "Sports Day is fun. I'm going to see it with my friend Carla."

The ladybug flew down from Bella's nose and landed on top of the bluebell in front of her.

"How can I go when I look like this?"

Bella stared at the ladybug. "What's wrong?" she asked. "You look all right to me."

The ladybug sighed. "How many spots can you see?"

Bella peered closely. The little insect was as red and shiny as a juicy apple. Right in the middle of her back was a single black spot.

"Oh!" Bella said. "You have only *one* spot."

The ladybug's eyes filled with

tears. "Exactly! How can I go to Sports Day with just one spot? I'll look stupid!"

"It's a *nice* spot," Bella said.

The ladybug shook her head. "Proper ladybugs have lots of spots. I'm the only ladybug I know with just one. My family knows I'm different. They love me all the same. I don't even mind when my friends call me One-Spot. But"—the ladybug stopped to catch her

breath—"if I go to Sports Day,
*all* the insects in Misty Wood will
see me, and they'll laugh." The
ladybug's lip trembled. Her eyes
were bright with tears.

"Don't be sad," Bella said.

"How can I not be sad?" the ladybug replied.

Bella's violet eyes lit up. "I know! I'll help you find some more spots."

The ladybug looked confused. "How will you do that?"

"Hmm. Let me think." Bella crouched down and leaned her head to one side to help her brain work better. She wiggled her nose— sometimes that helped her think.

Suddenly, her whiskers twitched, and she hopped in the air.

"We need a song! I never do anything without a song."

Bella hopped and skipped around the little insect. Then she started to sing, thumping her paws on the ground to keep the rhythm.

*This ladybug needs some spots.*

*Hoppity, hoppity, hop!*

*We're going to find lots and lots.*

*Hoppity, hoppity, hop!*

*Hopping here and hopping there,*

*Hopping, bopping everywhere!*

*She'll be happy when she's got*

*LOTS AND LOTS OF SPOTS!*

"How was that?" Bella asked, giving an extra-bouncy hop as she finished singing. But there was no reply.

The ladybug had vanished!

## CHAPTER THREE

# Wanted: Spots!

"Don't worry, I'm up here!" a little voice cried from high in the air.

Bella peered into the sky.

The ladybug zoomed down past

her nose. "Wheeee!" she squealed, whizzing up again and making a big circle in the air.

"Wow! Loop-the-loops!" Bella cried, sitting up on her hind legs to watch as the tiny insect whizzed around again.

"I always do loops when I'm happy," said the ladybug, swooping down to rest on a bluebell stem. "I'm so excited you're going to help me. Thank you!"

"You're welcome. I'm excited,
too! By the way, my name is
Bella."

"I'm Lexi!" said the ladybug.

"It's lovely to meet you, Lexi. Right. Let's get started," Bella said.

"Hurray!" said Lexi, swinging from the bluebell stem, her eyes shining.

"Now, let me think." Bella tilted her head and wiggled her nose. "Spots . . . spots," she muttered to herself. "Where can we find some spots?"

Then she jumped up, her long whiskers quivering. "I know! My

best friend, Carla, has lots of beautiful spots. Let's go and ask her where they came from."

Lexi didn't say anything. She looked down at the ground.

"What's wrong?" Bella asked.

"I'm scared." Lexi's voice shook as she spoke. "We might bump into some of the insects who are going to Sports Day. They'll laugh at my one stupid spot, and . . . oh . . . it'll be awful!"

"Don't be afraid!" Bella said kindly. "We'll think of something." She leaned her head to one side again to think. How could they find Carla without anyone seeing Lexi? One of Bella's long ears flopped down and touched the ground.

Bella grinned. She had the answer! "Look, Lexi." Bella lifted her silky ear with her paw. "You can hide under here."

"Ooh, yes!" Lexi flew over and

crawled under Bella's ear. There
was lots of room, and as Lexi
nestled into Bella's soft fur, she felt
cozy and safe.

Bella gently flapped her golden
fairy wings and floated up into the
sunlight. She headed for the edge
of Misty Wood, where the cobwebs
hung thickly on the tall hedgerows.
That was where Carla would be.

Carla looked very surprised when

she saw Bella. "I thought you were going to Bluebell Glade," she said.

"I was—and I did—but I need to ask you something," Bella replied, fluttering down to land beside her friend. "Something really important."

Carla blinked her big green eyes. She looked puzzled. "All right. Just let me finish this."

Bella watched as Carla hung some of her dewdrops on a cobweb

that stretched along the top of
the hedge. The dewdrops shone
and sparkled, and the spider silk
glittered like a diamond necklace.

"What's happening?" Lexi
whispered. "I can't see." She started
wriggling about under Bella's ear.

"Shh!" Bella whispered. "And
keep still. You're tickling me!"

Carla glanced around. "I'm
not tickling you," she said, looking
confused. "How can I be tickling

you when I'm over here hanging up my dewdrops?"

Bella frowned. "No, not you. I . . . I meant my nose was tickling me. I think I need to sneeze." She rubbed her nose with her front paws.

"Are you okay?" Carla's big eyes widened with concern.

"I'm fine. Look." Bella hopped and skipped a couple of steps, just to prove it.

Carla placed her basket on the

mossy ground. "So, what did you want to ask me?"

"Well, we . . . I mean . . . *I* was wondering, where did you get your spots?" Bella asked.

"My spots?" Carla looked down

45

at the chocolate-colored markings
on her snowy white fur.

"Yes. They're so lovely. Where
did they come from?" Bella said.

"I've always had them, ever
since I was a tiny kitten," Carla
replied. "I've no idea where they
came from."

Bella heard Lexi sigh under
her ear.

"Don't worry," Bella whispered
to Lexi. "We'll find someone in

Misty Wood who can help."

"Help with what?" Carla stared
at Bella.

"Oh, nothing! Thank you for
trying, Carla. See you soon!" Bella
hopped away along the hedgerow.

"Bye!" called Carla, still looking
confused. "See you later, at Insect
Sports Day!"

Bella patted her ear to check
that Lexi was safely tucked away.
Then, with a rustle and a shimmer

47

of her golden wings, she took off
and soared toward the middle of
Misty Wood.

Honeydew Meadow spread out
below them. Bella could see some
golden Pollen Puppies darting
about like sunbeams as they did
their special job: spreading the
pollen to make the flowers grow.
But not one of the puppies had any
spots.

Next, Bella flew toward

Dandelion Dell. In the clearing
next to the dell, she caught sight
of something moving. It was a

graceful Dream Deer with long legs and huge eyes. His smooth brown coat and gauzy wings were dappled all over with silvery spots.

"I think I've found someone!" Bella cried. "Hang on tight, Lexi!"

Bella fluttered down to where the deer was nibbling on the sweet spring grass. Surely if anyone could help Lexi, it would be a Dream Deer.

## CHAPTER FOUR

# Daydreaming

The Dream Deer lifted his nose
from the grass and gazed at Bella
with kind brown eyes.

"Are you searching for a dream,

little bunny?" he asked Bella.

Like all the fairy animals in Misty Wood, the Dream Deer had their own special job. When the other animals were sleeping, the deer brought them happy dreams.

Bella yawned. The deer's voice was so soft and gentle it made her feel like taking a nap. She flopped down on the grass.

"Oh, dear," she said. "I think I'm falling asleep."

"No!" Lexi cried in her ear.

"Please do," the deer said in his velvety voice. "I have a lovely dream for you."

"Noooo!" Lexi cried again.

But as Bella's eyes closed, the ladybug's voice began to fade. The Dream Deer's magic was working.

Bella dreamed she was opening buds high in the treetops. But she'd never seen flowers like these before.

They were huge white blossoms, hanging like brightly shining moons.

"Please don't go to sleep!" a little voice squeaked in Bella's ear. "What about my spots?"

But Bella was lost in her dream, and she didn't hear Lexi at all.

Now she could see that the white flowers were dotted with gold and yellow and silver. They had lots and lots of beautiful spots.

54

"Spots!" Bella called out, opening her eyes and jumping up.

"Hurray!" Lexi cried.

The deer looked at Bella, surprised. "Didn't you like your dream?" he asked.

"I loved it," Bella told him. "But I can't sleep now. I need to find some spots. Where did *your* spots come from?"

The deer flicked his tail and turned his long neck to look at the

silvery spots on his fur and wings.

"I don't know," he said.

"They've always been there."

Bella heard Lexi give another

sad little sigh in her ear. Bella

tried not to show the deer how

56

disappointed she was. "Oh well. Thank you anyway. And thanks for the lovely dream."

The deer smiled warmly. "I'm very sorry I wasn't able to help you," he said. "I do hope you find some spots, whatever they are for." Then he leaped gracefully into the air and soared away.

"What are we going to do now?" Lexi whispered.

"I don't know," Bella said. She

was beginning to feel a *tiny* bit worried, too.

"You could try another song," Lexi suggested.

"Good idea." Bella jumped up and began hopping along a little path that led through the trees. Lexi snuggled back under Bella's ear. After a moment, Bella began to sing.

*Hop-a-long, hop-a-long,*
   *hoppity-hop!*

*We're looking for someone to give*

*us some spots.*

*A Dream Deer couldn't help us,*

*And neither could a kitten!*

*So we're searching the wood*

*For where they are hidden!*

Bella kept hopping and singing.

The path led deep into the Heart of Misty Wood. The trees grew close together, and the ferns and moss were thick and green.

Bella felt a little afraid. Apart from her song, this part of the wood was silent. There was no one around, and no sign of *any* spots!

*Oh, dear. I must be going the wrong way*, Bella thought.

She was about to turn and hop back when a ray of sunshine lit the

path ahead. The trees thinned as she hopped into a clearing.

Bella came to a halt, her heart beating fast. There was a ring of bright red toadstools in the clearing.

"Why have you stopped?" Lexi asked.

Bella raised her ear so that

Lexi could see the toadstools.

"Mushrooms?" Lexi said. "How can mushrooms help us?"

"They're not mushrooms. They're *toadstools*!" Bella explained.

Lexi was very puzzled.

"It's a magic toadstool ring!" Bella whispered. "A place where wishes come true!"

And without another word, she hopped out of the trees and flew straight to the middle of the ring.

CHAPTER FIVE

# Magic Toadstools

It was very quiet in the middle of
the toadstool ring. There were no
birds singing, and even the leaves in
the trees had stopped rustling. Bella

gave a little shiver, but she knew she
must be brave. She raised her ear
right up.

"Come and sit beside me," she
whispered to Lexi.

"Why?" Lexi asked.

"We need to close our eyes,"
Bella explained. "Then I'll make a
wish for you to have some spots."

"Oh, I hope it works," breathed
Lexi.

Bella closed her eyes tight and

thought for a moment. As soon as the words came into her head, she began to sing.

*Lexi's only got one spot,*

*Which makes her feel so sad.*

*But grant my wish, kind toadstools,*

*And she'll be very glad!*

Bella stopped singing and listened. There was still no sound. Not even the faintest breeze or quietest birdsong. But then . . . *swoosh!*

Something ruffled against her.

"What's that?" Lexi squeaked.

*Swish! Swoosh!*

There it was again. It felt as if a big, soft brush was stroking Bella's fur.

"Don't move!" Bella whispered to Lexi. "It's the magic. You have to keep your eyes closed."

Suddenly, the swooshing stopped. Everything was quiet.

Bella opened one eye and saw

the ring of toadstools. Then she opened her other eye.

"Oh no!" she gasped when she saw Lexi.

"Oh no!" squeaked Lexi when she saw Bella.

"What's wrong?" they both said at exactly the same time.

"You've got spots!" Bella said. "But—"

"So have you," interrupted Lexi. "Big white ones!"

67

Bella stared at the ladybug. "Yours are white, too!"

"They can't be!" Lexi cried.

"It's true," Bella said. "Let's go look in that puddle over there."

They fluttered over to look at their reflections in the water.

"It *is* true!" Lexi said. "I've got lots and lots of white spots. But they should be *black*."

Bella gazed at her friend. The ladybug did look strange, with

one big black spot and lots of little white ones. Then Bella leaned over to look at her own reflection.

"Oh my!" she exclaimed. There were big white blobs all over her silky gray fur. She didn't look like her usual self at all.

Lexi started to cry. Tiny trails of tears glimmered as they trickled down her face. "I c-can't go to Sports Day like this! What are we going to do?"

69

"Don't worry," Bella said. "This
toadstool ring is definitely magic,

but I must have sung the wish wrong. Let me try again."

Bella started flying back toward the ring, but Lexi stayed where she was.

"Why aren't you coming?" Bella asked.

"The magic might go wrong again," Lexi replied. "I might end up with purple spots. Or spots every color of the rainbow. And that would be even worse!"

"I'm sure that won't happen," Bella said, flying back over to Lexi. "I just have to get the wish right. That's all."

Lexi gave a little nod and fluttered back to the toadstool ring.

When they were both in the ring again, they closed their eyes. Bella tilted her head, wiggled her nose, and then started singing.

*I should have asked for black spots!*
*Can the white ones disappear?*

*Lexi needs some black ones.*

*Oh, I do hope you can hear!*

Misty Wood was silent again. Had the song worked? Bella opened one eye to take a peek. Lexi's spots were still white! The toadstools had worked their magic the first time—why weren't they listening now? Bella took a deep breath and bellowed at the top of her voice.

*Listen, toadstools, in your ring,*

73

*Can't you hear me when I sing?*

*Lexi needs some BLACK SPOTS*

*And—*

"There's no need to shout," a deep voice interrupted.

Bella's fur stood on end, and Lexi squeaked with fright. They both kept their eyes shut tight. Maybe the magic was working?

"I don't do black spots," the voice said. "I do only white."

*That doesn't sound very magical,*

74

Bella thought. She opened her eyes.

A large red fox was sitting in front of them. He was holding a lily pad full of white paint.

75

"Are you *sure* you do only white spots?" Lexi said.

"Quite sure," said the fox, nodding.

"Sorry," said Bella. "But Lexi needs *black* spots."

"Yes," said Lexi. "I'm a ladybug, you see."

The fox stood up and shook himself. "Watch this," he said. Then he trotted over to the edge of the ring with his lily pad. He dipped

his tail in the paint and dabbed one of the red toadstools until it was covered with white spots.

"See?" he said. "That's my job. Putting the white spots on the toadstools."

"Gosh, that looks lovely," Bella said. "Much better than plain red toadstools."

"Thanks," the fox said with a smile. "I'm really sorry I'm not able to help you. And don't worry.

The spots will wash off. I have to repaint these toadstools every time it rains."

He picked up his lily pad and moved on to the next toadstool.

"Good-bye, Mr. Fox. Thank you for trying to help us," Bella said. "Come on, Lexi."

"Where are we going?" Lexi asked as she settled down in Bella's soft fur.

"Moonshine Pond," Bella told

her. "We'll wash away these white spots, and then we'll think of what to do next."

"Okay!" squeaked Lexi as the bunny opened her golden wings and fluttered into the air. "Let's go!"

CHAPTER SIX

# Moonshine Pond to Heather Hill

"The pond looks so bright and beautiful today," Bella cried as she spotted the gleaming water through

the trees. "The Moonbeam Moles have been busy."

Every night, the moles caught moonbeams and dropped them into Moonshine Pond to make it glow like the moon itself.

Bella landed on the grassy bank. "Okay, Lexi, time to wash off those spots," she called, raising her ear so Lexi could fly out.

Lexi landed on the bank and looked down at the silvery water.

"What if they don't wash off?" she said nervously.

"Oh, I'm sure they will. Look." Bella dipped a paw in the edge of the pond. The fox was right—the water washed the white blobs clean away.

"Yippee!" Lexi cried, and she did a quick loop-the-loop before diving headfirst into the water.

Bella hopped in, too, and splashed and splashed until all the spots were gone.

"That's better!" she cried,

leaping onto the bank and shaking

out her fur and wings.

"You look like a proper Bud Bunny again!" said Lexi, crawling out from the water. "Are my spots gone, too?"

"They are," Bella replied. "Only the black one's left."

"I'd better dry myself off," Lexi said. She flew up into the air, whirring her little wings as she loop-the-looped.

Bella sat down on the grass. She felt really sad that she hadn't been

able to help Lexi, but it was lovely to rest in the sunshine. She could feel the warm rays drying her fur.

"Wheeee!" came Lexi's voice from high in the air.

Bella looked up and smiled. Lexi must be feeling very happy that the white spots were gone. She was loop-the-looping again and again.

Then Bella saw a large yellow butterfly fluttering through the

trees. It was the same one she and Carla had met that morning.

"Hello again!" the butterfly said, landing on the grass.

"Hello, Mr. Butterfly. I thought you were going to Sports Day," Bella said.

"It's just about to start," the butterfly explained. "As chief steward, it's my job to make sure no insects get left behind. I wouldn't want anyone to miss it!"

Then he saw Lexi loop-the-looping.

"My, oh my, little ladybug, what wonderful flying!" he called. "With talent like that, you should be racing in Sports Day. Quick, come with me."

Bella was about to explain that Lexi was shy, but it was too late. The butterfly had leaped into the air.

"Oh, no, no, no!" squealed Lexi,

87

zooming up to the top of her loop as the butterfly approached.

But the butterfly was in such a hurry that he didn't hear her. He scooped Lexi up in his long legs and swooped off through the trees.

Bella, confused, twitched her nose. Everything had happened so quickly. One moment Lexi was happily loop-the-looping, and the next moment she was gone!

Bella whirled her shining golden

wings and flew after the butterfly as fast as she could.

"Don't worry, Lexi!" she shouted as she took off. "I'm coming!"

"Wow!" Bella gasped as she saw Heather Hill.

Everything was ready for Insect Sports Day. There was a circular flying track for the June bugs and the ladybugs, with lots of obstacles for them to get over. Flowers had been laid out to make a nectar-gathering marathon for the bees. There was a high jump for the grasshoppers and a cobweb trapeze for the spiders, and some fireflies were marking out an area in the sky for the butterflies' races.

All around the edge of the arena, fairy animals were taking their places, excitedly waiting for Sports Day to begin. The Pollen

90

Puppies were wagging their tails
so fast they blurred. The Stardust
Squirrels were scampering about,
sprinkling stardust until the heather
glittered silver in the sun.

Bella saw a group of Cobweb
Kittens sitting under a large oak
tree. She wondered if her friend
Carla was here already, but she
couldn't stop and check now. She
had to find out if Lexi was okay.

Bella dived into the crowd of

insects who were hurrying about and pushed her way to the front.

She spotted the yellow butterfly at the start of the flying track. Lexi was with him. She looked scared. Bella wished there was something she could do to help her.

Three other young ladybugs were there, too. They were wearing leg bands with numbers on them— one, two, and three.

Ladybug Three was holding a

fourth band and looking worried.

"What shall we do?" he said to the

butterfly. "The fourth member of

95

our team has hurt his wing and won't be able to race."

"Aha!" the butterfly said. "No need to worry. It just so happens that I have found a ladybug so fast, so fantastic, and so fabulous at flying, she will make the perfect fourth member of your team." The butterfly twirled his antennae with a flourish. "This is Lexi. She is your new Number Four!"

"Yay!" The three ladybugs

whooped and buzzed excitedly.

Bella held her breath. She wondered if they would notice that Lexi had only one spot. Lexi was obviously wondering the same thing. She was hopping from one tiny foot to the other. But the other ladybugs didn't seem to notice at all.

"You're the most important member of the team," the butterfly told Lexi. "Number Four does the last lap of the race. If you win,

97

you'll be the star of Sports Day."

He fixed the number four band onto Lexi's leg. Lexi fluttered her wings nervously.

"The Obstacle Relay Race is on!" the butterfly cried. "Ladybugs against June bugs. Good luck!"

"Be brave, Lexi," Bella called. "You'll be great!" She hoped Lexi could hear her.

Just then, a baby caterpillar who was sitting on his moth

mommy's back noticed Lexi
waiting behind the start line.

"Look!" he said in a loud,
surprised voice. "That ladybug's
got only one spot!"

Bella groaned. Poor Lexi!
Lexi was quite close to the little
caterpillar, so she must have heard
what he'd said. But there was
nothing Bella could do.

The yellow butterfly was giving
his instructions to the ladybug

team. He held up a grass seed. "Here's your baton. Pass it to the next ladybug as you finish your lap. If you don't, the team will be disqualified."

Ladybug One took the grass seed in his antennae and fluttered up to the start. He lined up next to a small green June bug.

"Ready?" the butterfly asked.

The ladybug and the June bug nodded.

"Get set!" called the butterfly.

A bumblebee flew forward.

"*ZZZZZ!* GO!" she buzzed.

The two little insects flew off so fast that their wings began to hum. They headed for the first obstacle—a huge pile of sticks.

Bella looked back at Lexi and saw that her friend was sitting on the ground, looking very frightened indeed. With a quick hop and a skip, Bella made her way to the

101

front until she was standing right next to Lexi.

"Wow, this is so exciting!" Bella said. "Three laps and then it'll be your turn."

Quivering with fear, Lexi held her front legs over her eyes. "I can't do it, Bella," she said. "Everyone will laugh at me. What am I going to do?"

102

CHAPTER SEVEN

# Loop-the-Loop

The yellow butterfly hovered in the
air. He was holding a bright orange
mushroom shaped like a trumpet.
"They're off!" he shouted into the

mushroom. His voice echoed all over Heather Hill. "The ladybug and the June bug are coming up to the first obstacle, the sticks! And they're over!"

Bella looked down at Lexi.

Lexi was still covering her eyes.

The rest of the crowd was very excited. All the ladybugs jumped up and down. "That's our boy!" they yelled.

The June bugs jumped up and

down, too. "Faster!" they shouted
to the green June bug. "Go, go, go!"

Behind her, Bella could hear
the Pollen Puppies yelping with
joy. She looked back at the race.

105

The June bug was just entering the cobweb tunnel.

"Touch those sides, and you'll stick fast!" the butterfly cried.

Bella's whiskers twitched with excitement as the ladybug reached the tunnel.

"Number One's just about to go in," she said to Lexi, "but he's behind the June bug."

"The June bug's way out in front! He's at the last obstacle!"

shouted the butterfly. "There he goes, up the helter-skelter tree!"

"This bit looks really exciting," Bella said to Lexi as the June bug flew around and around between the branches of a tall tree. But Lexi still wouldn't uncover her eyes.

Bella's heart pounded as the June bug bumped into some branches. But he made it to the finish safely and back to the starting line.

"Now June Bug Two's got the baton, and he's still in the lead!" the butterfly shouted.

Ladybug One was a long way behind as he flew up to the start, holding out the grass seed for Ladybug Two.

The second ladybug was faster than the first. She raced through the tunnel so quickly, she came out ahead of the June bug!

Bella thumped her paws in glee.

108

Ladybug Two was brilliant!

"Look, Lexi!" Bella begged.

"She's overtaken the June bug!"

But Lexi still wouldn't look.

The butterfly roared into his

mushroom trumpet: "Ladybug Two

is coming up to the finish. Now
Ladybug Three is off!"

Bella turned to Lexi. "You're
next! Come on!"

"No, I can't!" squeaked Lexi.

Bella's ears drooped in despair.
How, oh, how could she get Lexi to
race? Then she had an idea. Bella
snuggled up close to her friend,
and she started singing a new song,
very softly, so that only Lexi could
hear.

*It doesn't matter a jot*

*That you've got only one spot.*

*You can do it if you try—*

*All you have to do is fly!*

Lexi opened her eyes and stared at Bella. "Do you really think I can do it?"

Bella smiled and nodded. "Of course you can. You're wonderful at flying."

Lexi gave a big sigh. Then, very slowly, she stepped up to the

starting line. Everyone could see her one black spot now.

Bella knew how afraid Lexi was that everyone would laugh. But the crowd wasn't looking at Lexi. Everyone was pushing forward to see Ladybug Three as she finished her lap. She was out in front!

"Come on, ladybugs!" yelled the butterfly. "Number Three's in the lead! All she has to do is hand over to Ladybug Four. Oh no!"

There were so many creatures milling around at the starting line that Ladybug Three couldn't see who to pass the baton to. She circled in the air, searching for the fourth member of the team.

"This way!" Bella shouted. "Look for One-Spot Lexi!"

The sun shone down on Lexi and her single black spot. *Now* Ladybug Three knew who to head for! She whizzed down toward

Lexi, holding out the grass-seed baton.

"Go, Lexi, go!" shouted Bella with a big grin.

Lexi seized the baton in her antennae and zoomed away. She was over the sticks in a flash, with a spectacular loop-the-loop.

The crowd went wild, cheering and clapping, and the Pollen Puppies wagged their tails faster than ever.

"We're on the last lap now. The June bugs are in the lead again. But just look at that!" howled the butterfly. "The ladybug's at the tunnel already!"

Lexi shot through the cobweb tunnel like an arrow. She was catching up to June Bug Four!

"This is amazing!" the butterfly gabbled. "Just look at One-Spot Lexi! She's loop-the-looping all the way up the helter-skelter tree!"

115

"Go, Lexi, *go*!" yelled Bella.

"I've never seen anything like it!" the butterfly shrieked. "She's fantabulous! She's brilltastic! She's right behind the June bug!"

Bella hopped up and down, clapping her front paws as Lexi

hurtled toward the finish. Now she
was in front of the June bug!

"Go, One-Spot Lexi! Go, go,
*go*!" roared the crowd.

Lexi shot across the finish line.

"Yes!" cried the butterfly,
throwing his trumpet into the air

and catching it. "She's done the fastest time ever! A Misty Wood record. The ladybugs have won!"

"I did it!" Lexi panted, circling down to land on the grass in front of Bella.

"You won! You won!" Bella was so proud of her new friend. "You're a star, Lexi!"

The rest of the ladybug team came up to congratulate Lexi.

"You were incredible!" Ladybug

One said. "We'd never have won without you."

The yellow butterfly called the team over to collect their prizes. He gave each ladybug an acorn cup full of golden honey.

"Well done, One-Spot Lexi," he said.

Lexi blushed even redder. She took her honey and hurried back to Bella.

"Let's get away before they

start laughing at my spot,"
she said, looking around at the
spectators who were still buzzing
with excitement about the race.

The two friends fluttered their
wings and drifted away over the
heather, looking for somewhere
quiet. But everywhere they went,
insects and fairy animals flew up to
congratulate Lexi.

"Hello!" called a Moss Mouse.
"I loved your loop-the-loops!" He

tried a clumsy loop of his own
before flying off.

"Mmmarvelous!" droned
a furry bee. "Bbbbessst race
evvvvverr!" Then she buzzed away,
searching for a flower.

"They're not laughing at me!"
Lexi said, looking very surprised.

"Why would they laugh?" Bella
said with a smile. She saw a patch
of grass between the heather plants.
"Let's go and sit over there so you

can eat some of your prize honey."

"You have to have some, too," Lexi said. "If it wasn't for you, I'd never have been brave enough to race."

They flew down and were just dipping into the acorn when a very small ladybug peeped at them through the heather stalks.

He looked at Lexi shyly. "Hello, Lexi. You're my hero," he mumbled, then darted away.

Lexi stared after him. Then she looked at Bella, puzzled. "Why would he say that I'm his hero?"

"Because you won the race for the ladybug team," Bella said. "And it wasn't *just* because you're so good at flying."

"What do you mean?" Lexi asked.

Bella licked a drop of delicious honey from her paw. "Well, if you weren't One-Spot Lexi, Ladybug

123

Three would never have known who to pass the baton to."

Lexi looked thoughtful. Then her eyes began to shine. "You mean . . . it was a *good* thing that I have only one spot?"

Bella nodded. A smile spread slowly across Lexi's face, and she zoomed up into the air in a happy loop-the-loop. "Maybe being different isn't so bad after all," she called down to Bella. "Wheeeeeee!"

124

There was a shimmer of silver wings above the heather, and Carla the Cobweb Kitten fluttered down to join them.

"Hello, Bella! I've been looking for you everywhere," she said. "Did you see the Obstacle Relay Race? It was amazing!"

"Yes," Bella said proudly. She nodded at Lexi. "My new friend here just won it."

"Oh, wow!" Carla looked at

Lexi with admiration. "You were brilliant. I wish I could do loop-the-loops like you."

"I can teach you if you like," Lexi said shyly.

"Ooh, really?" Carla fluttered her silver wings excitedly. "I would love that!"

Carla turned back to Bella. "Are you still trying to find out where spots come from?"

Bella looked at Lexi.

Lexi smiled and shook her head. She was happy just the way she was.

"Not anymore," Bella said, winking at Lexi. "No need for more spots here!"

127

The sun was starting to hide his face behind the trees of Misty Wood, and the sky was turning golden pink. The warm spring day was coming to an end. It was nearly time to go home.

"Thank you, Bella," said Lexi. "Your songs have really helped me today."

"You're welcome," Bella said. "In fact . . ."

Bella began hopping around

Lexi and Carla as she started
singing another song.

*Making friends with you*

*Has been the best thing by far.*

*One-Spot Lexi,*

*The loop-the-loop star!*

# Misty Wood Word Search

Can you find all these words from
the story in this fun word search?

BELLA     HOP     RACE
BUNNY     LEXI     SKIP
FlOWER     PETAL     WINGS

X T O N F B U N N Y L V T
R P E R B R A C E E A L C
C J R B H V F A W T X H K
H N V S D G L H L I H O P
W A D G F L O W E R N I M
D Z E C E R L I T K G Q
Y D X B M X W G K S L F S
B N U V E I E W P H A N K
P E T A L E K L U L L L P

# Help Bella finish her song!

Bella loves singing about Misty Wood! She was making up a new song when she had to hop off to Bluebell Glade to open some buds.

Help Bella finish her song in the lines below.

*I love skipping over the hill.*
*To skip, skip, skip*
*Gives me a thrill!*

*I love hopping in the sun.*
*To hop, hop, hop*
*Is so much fun!*

_____

_____

_____

Help Lexi find her way
to the finish line.
Watch out for dead ends!

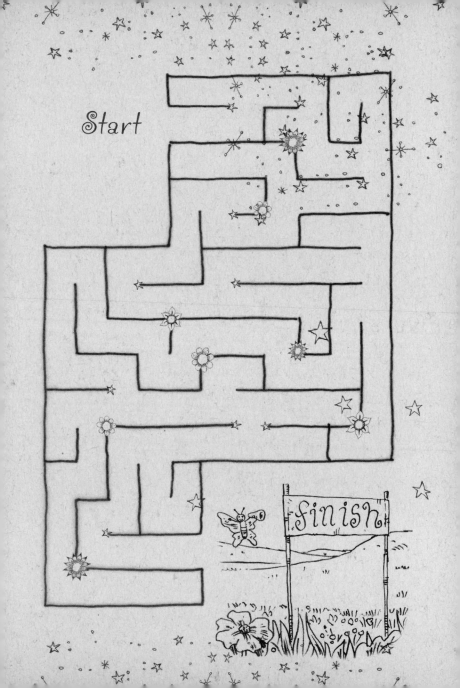

Start

finish

# Fairy Animals
## of Misty Wood

# Paddy the Puppy

### Lily Small

Henry Holt and Company
New York

*With special thanks to Thea Bennett*

Henry Holt and Company, LLC
*Publishers since 1866*
175 Fifth Avenue
New York, New York 10010
mackids.com

Library of Congress Cataloging-in-Publication Data
Small, Lily.
Paddy the puppy / Lily Small. — First American edition.
pages cm. — (Fairy animals of Misty Wood ; 3)
"Originally published in Great Britain in 2013 by Egmont UK Limited."
Summary: Paddy the Pollen Puppy is so excited about today being his
birthday that he causes all sorts of trouble. Includes activities.
Paper Over Board ISBN 978-1-250-11396-2 — Paperback ISBN 978-1-250-11397-9
[1. Fairies—Fiction. 2. Dogs—Fiction. 3. Animals—Infancy—Fiction.
4. Birthdays—Fiction.] I. Title.
PZ7.S6385Pad 2015      [Fic]—dc23      2014047288

Henry Holt books may be purchased for business or promotional use.
For information on bulk purchases, please contact the Macmillan Corporate
and Premium Sales Department at (800) 221-7945 x5442
or by e-mail at specialmarkets@macmillan.com.

First American Edition—2015
Printed in the United States of America by
R. R. Donnelley & Sons Company, Harrisonburg, Virginia

Hardcover
1  3  5  7  9  10  8  6  4  2

Paperback
1  3  5  7  9  10  8  6  4  2

# Contents

## CHAPTER ONE

# A Very Exciting Morning

The sun had just come out to play above Misty Wood. Golden light danced all over the fresh green leaves of the trees and warmed the

beautiful flowers in the valleys and meadows. Everything was bursting with color.

In a cozy den under the Hawthorn Hedgerows, sparkling sunbeams nudged the mossy bed of Paddy the Pollen Puppy. Paddy was curled up in a furry ball, but he wasn't asleep. He'd been awake for *ages*. Today was his birthday, and he'd woken up early because he was so excited!

2

Paddy gazed around the den

at his mom; his dad; and his sister,

Pippa. Their floppy ears were lying

3

over their front legs, and their eyes were shut tight.

"Uhhh . . . hmmm," snored Paddy's dad, his fluffy tail twitching.

"Hmmm . . . uhhh," snored his mom, her silky ears quivering.

Paddy sighed. "I wish they'd wake up," he said to himself.

He got up and padded in a circle on his cushion of moss. Around and around and around.

Soon he felt dizzy, so he flopped
down again. He wriggled onto his
back and waved his white paws
in the air. Then he rolled over and
opened his glittery yellow wings.
He longed to fly across the den and
pounce on his mom's back, or give
his sister's tail a playful tug. But he
knew he shouldn't. They would be
grumpy if he woke them up early.

Like all the other fairy animals
in Misty Wood, Pollen Puppies had

an important job to do. They had
to flick pollen around the meadows
with their tails so that the flowers
could grow. It was very busy work,
so they needed plenty of sleep.

Paddy decided to think about
his birthday party while he waited
for everyone to wake up.

*It's going to be the best party
EVER*, he thought. *There'll be
hazelnut cake and elderflower juice and
sticky chestnut buns, and we'll collect*

*bubbles from Moonshine Pond and
blow them all over the wood!*

His tail began to wag at the
very idea.

*But, first of all, I'll have to
open my presents.* Paddy grinned,
showing his velvety pink tongue. *I
wonder what Mom and Dad got for me
this year. . . .*

He looked around the den. His
present must be hidden somewhere.
His mom, dad, and sister were all

7

sleeping on comfy moss cushions just like his. Maybe they'd slipped his present underneath one of them? But no—then it would get squashed. It must be hidden somewhere else.

Paddy stretched his wings and hopped off his cushion. He checked the beautiful cobweb that hung above the entrance to the den. It had already been decorated with sparkling dewdrops by the Cobweb Kittens. But apart from

the dewdrops glistening like jewels in the sun, the cobweb was empty. There was still no sign of Paddy's present.

"It must be here *somewhere*," Paddy muttered.

He put his shiny pink nose in the air and sniffed. But he couldn't smell anything apart from the sweet scent of flowers drifting down from the hedgerows.

He peered under the four

red-and-white toadstools that the
family sat on to eat their meals.

Nothing.

He nudged the pile of berries
that he and Pippa played catch
with.

Nothing there, either.

He peeped into the corner of
the den where his dad liked to sit
and chew sticks.

No. Not a thing!

Disappointed, Paddy wandered

back over to his cushion. As he

clambered onto it, he looked up.

And there, wedged into the bush

above his mom and dad and Pippa, was a very strange shape. Paddy stared at it. He was sure it hadn't been there before. His tail started wagging again.

It must be his present!

The mystery shape wasn't
too big, and it wasn't too small. It
wasn't exactly round, but it wasn't
square, either. Paddy started
panting with excitement, trying to
work out what it could be. Maybe
it was a soft, grassy brush to keep
his fur and wings tidy. Or maybe
it was a daisy-chain collar to wear
on special occasions—like birthday
parties. Or, best of all, maybe it
was a bone—a big, fat, juicy bone

that he could sit and chew on for weeks!

Paddy was so excited he wanted to jump up and down. He was so excited he wanted to bounce all around. He was so excited he wanted to spread his shimmering wings and buzz about like a Misty Wood bee. He just couldn't lie on his bed a moment longer. Paddy did a forward roll off his cushion and landed near his mom and dad.

Maybe if he got a little bit closer to the shape, he'd be able to sniff it . . . and then he might be able to guess what it was.

But the shape was hard to reach. It was sitting in the arch of a hawthorn branch that curved right over his mom and dad's bed. If he was going to get any closer to it, he'd have to climb up the branch, just a little bit. . . .

Paddy placed one paw on the

bottom of the branch. Then he hooked another paw a little higher.

*CREEEEEAAAAK* went the branch.

*Oh no!* thought Paddy.

But his mom and dad stayed asleep.

Paddy placed one of his front paws even higher still.

*CREEEEEAAAAK* went the branch.

*Oh no!* thought Paddy.

But his mom and dad still stayed asleep.

Breathing a sigh of relief, Paddy climbed even higher. Soon he'd be able to sniff the mysterious shape and find out what it was.

*CREEEEEAAAAK* went the branch.

*Oh no!* thought Paddy.

*CRACK* went the branch as it gave way.

*Oh no! Oh no! Oh no!* thought

Paddy as his paws slipped. He was so shocked he didn't even have time to flap his wings. Instead, he tumbled down and landed with a bump—right on top of his mom and dad!

## CHAPTER TWO

# *Aaahhh-choo!*

"Paddy!" his mom and dad cried
as they leaped out of bed, their fur
standing on end.

"Oops!" yelped Paddy. "Sorry,
Mom! Sorry, Dad!"

Paddy's dad had been so startled that he'd jumped onto Pippa's mossy bed.

"Help! The sky's fallen on top of me!" Pippa cried, waving her silky paws in the air.

"Don't worry, Pippa," her mom said. "It's only Dad."

"But why has *Dad* fallen on top of me?" Pippa asked sleepily.

Paddy's dad scampered back to his own cushion. "Because

Paddy fell on top of *me*," he said.
"What were you doing, Paddy?
You've woken all of us up!"

Paddy covered his eyes with
his paws. "I didn't mean to," he
whimpered. "I just saw the shape
up in the bush and I . . . I . . .
thought it might be . . . might
be . . . my . . ."

Paddy had given everyone
such a shock that he didn't even
dare mention his birthday. He

peeped between his paws, hoping

they weren't too upset.

"Ah, of course!" His mom

smiled. "You thought it was your

present! Happy birthday, Paddy!"

Paddy's dad smoothed

down his brown-and-cream fur

and patted Paddy's head. "Don't worry, Paddy. It was time to get up anyway. Happy birthday!"

Pippa's eyes were wide open now, and she bounded down from her cushion to give Paddy a lick. "It's your birthday!" she woofed. "I don't mind being woken up for that!" Pippa fluttered her yellow wings and clapped her paws together. "Happy birthday, Paddy!"

Paddy grinned. He wasn't in trouble after all! He glanced up at the strange shape again. "So . . . *is* that my present?" he panted eagerly.

His mom laughed. "No, it isn't. It's a bluebird's nest! And it's a good job you didn't manage to climb all the way up there, because it's full of eggs that are almost ready to hatch. Now, why don't we have some birthday breakfast?"

While their mom prepared some poppy-seed bread with homemade blackberry jam, Pippa and Paddy fetched their wooden plates. They scrambled up onto their toadstools, and soon they were digging in.

"As soon as you've finished, you have to go and do your special job," Paddy's mom said.

"But it's my birthday!" replied Paddy. "Can't I just have fun today?"

26

His mom smiled. "Pollen
Puppies *always* have fun, no matter
what they're doing."

"Hmm, yes, that's true,"

27

said Paddy, thumping his tail in agreement.

"And you have to go," said his dad, "because we need to get your party ready for when you come back."

"Oooh!" Paddy's tail began to wag even harder. "In that case, we'll go right now!"

Paddy and Pippa skipped out of their den into the bright sunshine. They opened their

glistening wings and flitted up over the hedges.

It was a beautiful summer's day. Little clouds were drifting across the sky like wisps of cotton candy. Paddy twitched his shiny pink nose and smiled. He could smell the sweet scent of hawthorn blossoms and dusky pink roses.

Down below, one of their neighbors, Heidi the Holly Hamster, was nibbling the leaves of

a holly bush into shape. She had to
start early, so they'd be ready for
Christmas.

"Good morning, Heidi!" Paddy
woofed. "It's my birthday!"

Heidi waved her tiny paw at
him. "I know! Happy birthday,
Paddy! See you at your party!"

Paddy and Pippa went on
their way. They flew over fairy
mushroom rings and a sea of
nodding dandelion clocks, then

# AAAHHH-CHOO!

floated down into Honeydew Meadow. The flowers were in full bloom—golden buttercups and purple foxgloves, fiery red poppies and soft, creamy lilies. They looked wonderful, and they were all laden with pollen. All they needed now was a flick from a Pollen Puppy's tail so that new flowers would grow!

When Paddy came in to land, a crowd of puppies gathered around him at once.

"Happy birthday!" they chorused. Then they turned up their noses and gave a happy, doggy howl. "Wahhooooooow!"

Paddy wanted to jump for joy.

The puppies set to work, bouncing through the meadow, wagging their tails. Paddy was so excited, his tail batted to and fro in a blur. His mom was right—his special job was fun! And it was more fun than ever on his birthday!

*Flick . . . flick . . . flick . . .*

*Flickflickflick.*

*Flickety-flickflickflick . . .*

Paddy had never wagged his tail so fast in his life!

And then he heard a noise.

"Aaahhh-choo!" sneezed his friend Petey, one of the other Pollen Puppies.

"Aaahhh . . . CHOO!" sneezed Polly, a pretty puppy with silky gray ears.

"AAAHHH . . . CHOO!
AAAHHH . . . CHOO!
AAAHHH . . . CHOO!"

Paddy looked around the meadow. His tail had flicked up clouds and clouds of pollen. All the other Pollen Puppies had stopped. Their sparkly wings were flat. Pippa was wiping her eyes with her paws. Others were spluttering and sneezing. Some were rubbing their little button

35

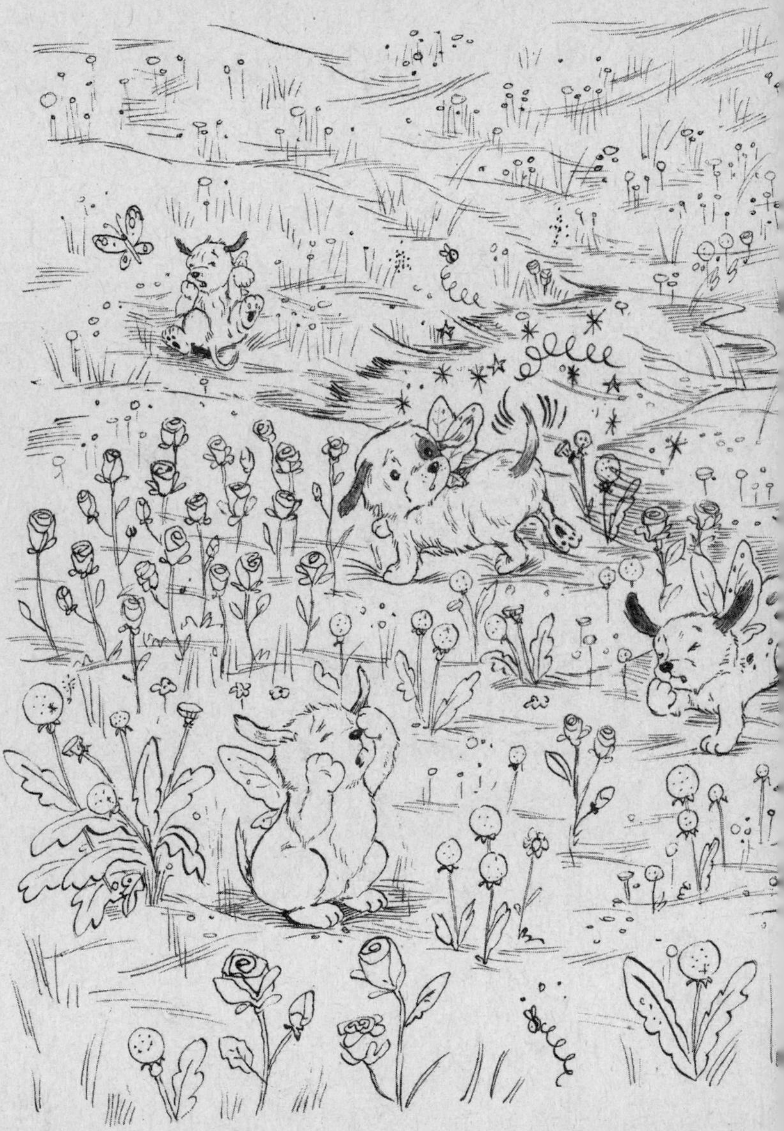

noses, trying to stop them from tickling.

"Paddy!" cried Petey. "You're working so fast that you've flicked ten times too much pollen! Aaahhh . . . choo!"

"Ooouuu!" howled Paddy in dismay. He looked back at his furry tail, which was still waving to and fro. "What do you think I should do?"

"We know you're excited about your birthday," a spotted puppy

named Pepper said. "So maybe you should use up some of your energy. Why don't you go flick pollen in Golden Meadow? Maybe by the time you've flown all the way there, your tail won't be wagging so hard."

"Oh yes," woofed Paddy. He shook his wings and did a little jig. "That's a great idea! Look out, Golden Meadow—the Birthday Pollen Puppy is coming your way!"

39

## CHAPTER THREE

# Happy Birthday to Me!

Paddy launched himself into the air. He waved good-bye to his friends in Honeydew Meadow and set off through the Heart of Misty

Wood. Paddy wanted to take the long way. It was lovely and cool among the trees. Paddy swooped around the towering tree trunks, practicing his flying skills.

"Happy birthday to me, happy birthday to meeeee!" he sang.

He zoomed up high to wag his tail at a woodpecker, who was peck-peck-pecking up in a tree. Then he flitted down to do a somersault over a rotting log.

41

He had just started humming his birthday tune again when he spotted a lovely big pile of leaves sitting under a beech tree. They looked *so* inviting! Paddy flew higher and hovered for a moment. "This will be fun!" he giggled to himself.

He pointed his shiny pink nose at the pile and began diving down. His wings whirred as they got faster and faster and faster. . . .

"Happy birthday, dear Paddy!" he warbled at the top of his voice as he skidded into the leaves at top speed. "Happy birthday to MEEEEEE!"

The leaves flew everywhere. Paddy rolled around in them, kicking his paws wildly. There were brown leaves, red leaves, yellow leaves, gold leaves. There were big leaves, small leaves, fat leaves, thin leaves.

"Oh, this is so much fun.

I'm having the best birthday ever!"

Paddy exclaimed as he flicked the leaves with his tail.

But then, suddenly, he heard a loud voice.

"HEY!"

Paddy jumped.

"HEY!" the voice called again, s ounding very angry.

Paddy looked around.

"Yes, YOU!"

Paddy brushed the leaves from his fur with his paws. Then he

plucked one leaf from between his wings. "Who is it?" he squeaked, feeling a teeny bit scared.

"It's Hattie the Hedgerow Hedgehog," said the voice. "And you've just spoiled my hard work!"

Oh, dear.

Oh dear, oh dear, oh dear!

All at once, Paddy understood why there had been such a big pile of leaves sitting in the middle of the wood. The Hedgerow Hedgehogs

had their own special job, just like all the other fairy animals in Misty Wood. They used their prickles to pick up leaves and keep the woods neat. Paddy clapped his paw to his mouth as Hattie fluttered out from behind the beech tree.

"I'm sorry," Paddy whimpered. "I didn't think the pile belonged to anyone."

Hattie landed on the ground in front of Paddy. Her prickles were

fluffed out in all directions, so she looked like a big spiky ball. She sighed. "What's your name, little Pollen Puppy?"

48

"I'm Paddy. And I'm really, truly sorry," whispered Paddy. He bent his head so that his ears drooped over his eyes. He even managed to stop wagging his tail, just to show how sorry he was.

"It took me all morning to get those cleaned up," Hattie said, looking sadly at the leaves. "And when I saw you messing them up— and singing a song while you did it—I thought you were ruining my

49

work on purpose." She rustled her rusty-brown wings and sniffed. "But you do look *very* sorry, I must say. What was that song you were singing?"

"Happy birthday," Paddy mumbled, "to—to me."

Hattie folded away her wings. "To you, eh?"

Paddy nodded his silky head. "Yes. You see, I was so excited about my birthday, and when I saw your

leaves I just thought they would be wonderful to play in," he explained. "I didn't mean to ruin anything, I really didn't. In fact, I'm on my way to do my own special job. Even though it's my birthday."

"I see." Hattie rubbed her chin with her delicate paw. Then she sighed. "Well, never mind. There aren't too many leaves at this time of year. I don't suppose it will take me long to tidy them up."

"Oh, but I can help you!" Paddy barked. He allowed his tail to give a little wag. "I have so much energy because it's my birthday, I have to use some of it up before I get to Golden Meadow. Otherwise I'll flick too much pollen and make all the other Pollen Puppies sneeze again!"

Hattie looked surprised. "That's nice of you." She smiled. "And it would be fun to have

52

someone to work with today. I'm all on my own in this part of the wood."

"Really?" said Paddy. "Come on, then, let's get started."

Paddy watched as Hattie fluffed out her prickles. Then she curled herself into a ball and rolled along the ground so that her prickles picked up the leaves. She looked so funny covered in leaves that Paddy started to laugh.

"You look more like a *hedge*
than a hedge*hog*!" He giggled.

Hattie grinned. "That's how
I'm supposed to look!" she told him,
shaking the leaves into a pile.
"Come on, now. You try!"

Paddy rolled through the
leaves, then peered around to look

at his back. It hadn't worked. Not a
single leaf had stuck to his soft fur.

"Oh, dear," he said. "I suppose
I'll have to find another way to
help you."

"Try collecting them in your
mouth instead," Hattie suggested.
So Paddy scampered off and

picked up a mouthful of leaves.
They felt so tickly against his
tongue he had to try really hard
not to laugh. He dropped the leaves
on top of Hattie's and then went
back for some more. He couldn't
collect as many leaves in his mouth
as Hattie could with her prickles,
so he had to run to and fro, to and
fro, his ears and wings flapping. It
was hard work! But at last all of the
leaves were in a neat pile again.

Hattie wiped her forehead with her paw. "Phew," she said. "We did it. Thank you, Paddy!"

"That's all right." Paddy grinned. "Now, I really must get to

Golden Meadow. But you'll come to my birthday party later, won't you? It's at Hawthorn Hedgerows."

"I'd love to!" said Hattie. "How exciting—a new friend and a birthday party, all in one day!"

CHAPTER FOUR

# Where's My Breakfast?

With a last wave to Hattie, Paddy
flew out of the Heart of Misty Wood
and into the open lands beyond.
Soon, he was soaring over Dewdrop

Spring, where the Cobweb Kittens collected their dewdrops in the morning.

The water was twinkling in the sun. It looked so magical that Paddy couldn't resist fluttering toward the surface to trail his paws in the cool, clear water. Blue and pink dragonflies skimmed along beside him, while bright green frogs hopped jauntily across the lily pads. Then Paddy spotted something

else. Something that made him think about his party. On the bank of the lake, next to an old, gnarled log, sat a little pile of acorns.

"Acorns!" Paddy cried. "The

61

best birthday parties *always* have acorns!"

He flew down and landed next to them. They were the biggest, roundest acorns he'd ever seen. He tried to remember the very best games to play with acorns. He loved *Hide the Acorn*, but he couldn't play that on his own. There was *Pass the Acorn*, but that needed friends, too. Then he remembered how one of the Bud

Bunnies had once shown him how to juggle. He imagined showing off to all his friends as they arrived at his party, juggling acorns high in the air.

"Up in the air, up in the air, juggle the acorns, if you dare!" he chanted.

Paddy grabbed a handful of acorns and began to throw them from one paw to another. But it was a lot harder to catch them than

he remembered. One of the acorns
flew up much too high. When it
came down again, it landed in
Dewdrop Spring with a big *PLOP!*

"Oh, dear," murmured Paddy.
"Never mind. There are still plenty
of acorns left."

He threw them up again.

"One, two, three, four, I'll catch
them with my tail and my nifty
paw!"

Paddy leaped around, trying to

catch the acorns. But as they came down, his paws got all tangled. *Thud! Bump!* went two of the acorns, landing on the bank and rolling into the water with a *plop*. As Paddy chased after them, a third acorn flew over his head and landed in the pond with a tinkly *splish*.

Then he heard a voice.

"Where's my breakfast?"

Paddy spun around. There,

sitting on the log, was a Stardust
Squirrel. Usually, Paddy would
have been very happy to see one.
He loved Stardust Squirrels. Their
fur glistened silver or dusky red,
and they had delicate wings to
match. When they shook their
bushy tails, they sent showers of
stardust all over Misty Wood. But
this one wasn't shaking his tail.
Instead, he was looking a little
angry.

"B-b-b-breakfast?" stuttered Paddy.

"Yes." The squirrel nodded his silvery head. "I put a perfect pile of delicious acorns right next to this log. And now they're all gone!"

"Oh, dear," said Paddy, hanging his head in shame.

The squirrel looked at Paddy, tilting his head to one side. "I don't suppose you might know what happened to them?"

Paddy laid his wings flat along his back and tucked his tail between his legs. He felt terrible.

"I'm so sorry," he said sadly. "I didn't know they were your breakfast. It's my birthday, you see, and I'm so excited—I just thought I'd see if I could juggle them. I thought it might be a fun trick for my party, but . . ." He looked sadly toward the lake.

The Stardust Squirrel raised
his tufty ears in disbelief. "You were
trying to juggle?" he squeaked.
"I've never seen a Pollen Puppy
juggle."

"No, well, it's not what we do
best," admitted Paddy.

"And what *do* you do best?"

Paddy cocked his head to one
side. "Wag our tails."

"That's what I thought," said
the Stardust Squirrel. Then he put

70

his paws to his mouth and started
to shake.

Paddy stared. The squirrel was
wobbling all over. Even his bushy
tail had joined in. It was sending
clouds of stardust into the air,
covering everything with glitter.

Then Paddy realized what
was happening. The squirrel was
laughing!

"Haw haw haw haw!" the
squirrel roared. "A Pollen Puppy

71

who thinks he can juggle! I've
never heard anything so funny in
the whole of Misty Wood!" Then
he stopped suddenly. "I'm sorry.
I don't mean to laugh at you—

especially on your birthday. It's just that . . . that . . ."

He tried to make his face serious, but he couldn't quite manage it. His nose and whiskers twitched, and his silver wings began to wiggle again.

Paddy thought of how all the acorns had plopped into the lake. It must have looked very funny. He began to giggle, too. Soon they were both laughing so hard that

73

they rolled around together on the bank of the lake, jiggling their wings and clutching their sides.

At last, they sat up and wiped their eyes. The Stardust Squirrel had covered the whole bank with stardust.

"Thank you, Pollen Puppy," he said. "You might have lost my breakfast, but you've made me laugh. What's your name?"

"Paddy. What's yours?"

"I'm Sammy," replied the
squirrel. "Now, I suppose I'd better
go and find some more acorns."

"Oh, no," said Paddy, wagging
his tail. "I should find them for
you." He pointed back toward the
Heart of Misty Wood. "There are
lots of big oak trees just over there.
Come on, I'll show you."

Together, they flexed their
wings and flew off toward the giant
oak trees. When they got there,

75

Paddy leaped and bounced around, sniffing out the plumpest, ripest acorns. Soon, Sammy had an even bigger pile than before!

"Thank you, Paddy!" said Sammy. "Looks like I've found a new friend as well as breakfast!"

"You're welcome," Paddy woofed. "Now, I'd better go and do my work in Golden Meadow. But will you come to my party later, at Hawthorn Hedgerows?"

Sammy twitched his bushy
tail, sprinkling stardust all over his
acorns. "Oh, yes please!" he cried.
"That would be great fun!"

## CHAPTER FIVE

# Paddy's Perfect Cushion

As Sammy started munching his breakfast, Paddy took off again for Golden Meadow, waving good-bye as he went. But his yellow wings began to feel heavy.

*Flap . . . flaaap . . . flaaaap . . .*

Paddy was flying slower
and slower. He'd woken up very
early and it had been such a busy
morning. Now he felt so tired that
he was starting to sink toward the
ground. "How will I ever reach
Golden Meadow?" he yelped to
himself.

Just below him, he saw a pretty
hill covered in nodding buttercups.
And right on top of the hill sat a

79

cushion. It was made of the softest, comfiest moss Paddy had ever seen, and it reminded him of his own snuggly bed.

*Ooh*, he thought. *That looks perfect for a nap. Just a quick nap . . .*

He floated down and flopped onto the cushion. He laid his head on the moss and closed his eyes. He was so tired that he fell asleep at once. And soon, he was dreaming.

It was a beautiful dream. He

was at the most wonderful birthday party in the world, and he was surrounded by presents. Everyone was cheering and clapping. The trees were decorated with daisy chains, and the air fizzed with stardust. Birds were twittering up in the branches, and all the fairy animals were singing birthday songs. Best of all, his mom and dad had given him the juiciest, tastiest bone he'd ever seen. Paddy was

dancing around it, wiggling his
body and waggling his tail. Then
all his Pollen Puppy friends linked
paws with him and joined in.

But something wasn't right.

"Oh! What have you done?"
he heard a squeaky voice say.

Paddy frowned. He tried to
grab his lovely bone, but when
his little jaws snapped shut, it
disappeared!

Paddy began to panic. He

83

couldn't possibly lose his birthday bone. . . .

"I said, what have you DONE?" the voice squeaked again, louder this time.

Paddy jumped. His eyes popped open. And there, tapping him on the nose with a little paw, was a Moss Mouse. He had pure white fur, the finest blue-and-white wings . . . and a big frown on his tiny face.

84

"Oh!" yelped Paddy as he remembered where he was. "I was dreaming about a bone. A beautiful, juicy bone . . ." He rubbed his eyes sadly.

"I know." The Moss Mouse sniffed.

"You know? How?" Paddy cocked his ears in surprise.

"Look what you've done to my cushion!" The Moss Mouse started hopping up and down. "I'm

85

Magnifico the Moss Mouse, and I
pride myself on my moss cushions.
This one was as round and smooth
as a springtime moon. *Now* see
what shape it is!"

Paddy jumped off the cushion.
He stared. The Moss Mouse was
right. It wasn't round anymore.
The cushion was shaped like a
huge bone!

"My tail must have wagged
it into that shape while I was

dreaming," Paddy said, still staring at the cushion in disbelief.

"Yes!" exclaimed Magnifico, folding his front paws. "That's exactly what it did."

Paddy felt very upset. His overexcited tail was causing all sorts of problems today. Moss Mice worked so hard to make all the lovely moss cushions in Misty Wood. They got up at dawn to hunt out the fluffiest moss from the shadiest valleys and the deepest dells. Then they spent hours patting it into shape.

"I'm really sorry," Paddy said. "It's my birthday, you see, and I'm

so excited. It wasn't just any old bone that I was dreaming about. It was a *birthday* bone."

"Oh!" said Magnifico, twitching his tiny pink nose. "Well, that does make a difference."

"Does it?" Paddy pricked his ears hopefully. "You mean you're not mad anymore? I'll help you get the cushion back into its proper shape, I promise!"

"Hmm. Well, let's see."

Magnifico walked all around the cushion. He looked at it one way. Then he looked at it another way. With a blurry buzz of his blue-and-white wings, he clambered up onto it. He ran to one end of the cushion and peered off the edge. Then he scampered to the other end and peered off that side, too. Paddy watched him, holding his breath.

At last, Magnifico bounced

back over to sit in front of Paddy
and began to chuckle.

"I think it's perfect," he said.

"Perfect?" Paddy wasn't sure
he'd heard correctly.

"I've never had a cushion in
the shape of a bone before," said
Magnifico. "Especially not in the
shape of a *birthday* bone. I'm going
to keep it, just as it is—in your
honor!"

"Ooooooh!" exclaimed Paddy.

"Thank you! Will it stay here for a long time?"

"Of course," said Magnifico. He smoothed back his whiskers proudly.

"I told you. I only make the very best quality cushions."

"So, I could come here and sit on it any time I like?" Paddy panted.

"I don't see why not," said Magnifico. "What's your name?"

"I'm Paddy."

"We can name it, if you like." Magnifico paused for a second. "How about, *Paddy's Birthday Bone Cushion?*"

"Oh, yes, yes, yes!" Paddy yapped. "Thank you!" He jumped up and padded the cushion with his paws. He would come and have a nap here as often as he could. He opened his wings and flapped back down to sit next to Magnifico. "In return, will you please come to my birthday party later? It's at Hawthorn Hedgerows."

Magnifico's shiny eyes lit up. "You're having a party?"

Paddy nodded.

"A real one, not a dream one?"

"Yes." Paddy's tail began wagging wildly.

"Wonderful," sighed Magnifico. "I love parties."

"This one's going to be the best in the world," Paddy told him. "Even better than the one in my dream!" He glanced up and saw that the sun was now high in the sky. "Ooh, I'd better

95

go, or I'll never get all my work done in Golden Meadow. See you later, Magnifico—and thank you again for my birthday cushion!"

CHAPTER SIX

# The Best Birthday Party Ever

Hovering over Golden Meadow
at last, Paddy was bursting with
happiness. The meadow's rainbow

colors shimmered in the sunshine, and he could just see the tips of other puppies' tails as they wagged their way around the swaying flower stems.

Paddy swooped down and landed softly. He was still excited, but he was careful to keep his tail much calmer now. *Flick . . . flick . . . flick . . .* it went. Pollen rose lightly and floated off on the gentle breeze, while other flowers opened their

petals wide to welcome it to a new home.

When half of the dandelion clocks had blown their seeds away, Paddy knew that it was time to go home. He had spread *lots* of pollen! He rose into the air and fluttered back toward Hawthorn Hedgerows.

*What an amazing day I've had!* he thought. He'd made three new friends—Hattie, Sammy, and Magnifico. He'd helped them tidy

leaves and collect acorns. He'd flicked more pollen than he'd ever thought a Pollen Puppy could. And he hadn't even had his birthday party yet! If only he didn't feel quite so tired . . .

As he floated down toward the hedgerows, Paddy's eyelids began to droop. He thought longingly of his little moss bed. Maybe he could have a snooze before all the fun began.

But then, just as he landed next to a purple toadstool, he heard a shout. A BIG shout.

"SURPRISE!"

Paddy peeped over the toadstool. Just ahead, in the clearing next to the hawthorn bushes, his whole family was waving and cheering. Pippa was bouncing up and down. And they weren't alone. All the other Pollen Puppies were there, and all his

friends from across Misty Wood.
There were Cobweb Kittens and
Holly Hamsters and Bud Bunnies
and even a couple of Moonbeam
Moles—and everyone knew that
moles preferred to go out in the
dark.

Then he heard a rustle of
rusty-brown wings.

His new friend Hattie the
Hedgerow Hedgehog was there!

Next, he saw a bushy silver tail,

which was sprinkling stardust
everywhere.

Sammy the Stardust Squirrel
was there!

Then he heard a cheeky squeak
at his feet. He looked down.

Magnifico the Moss Mouse
was there!

"Happy birthday, Paddy!"
everyone cried.

The glade had been decorated
just as Paddy had imagined in his

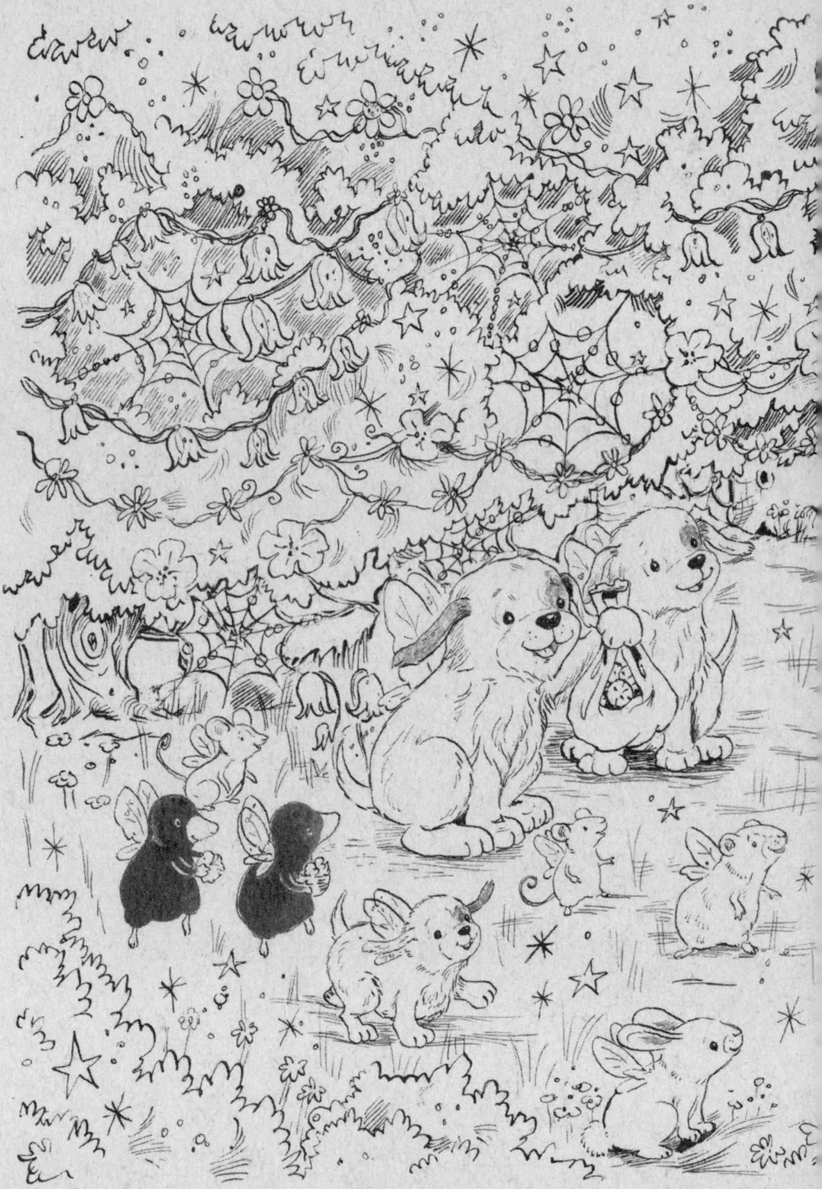

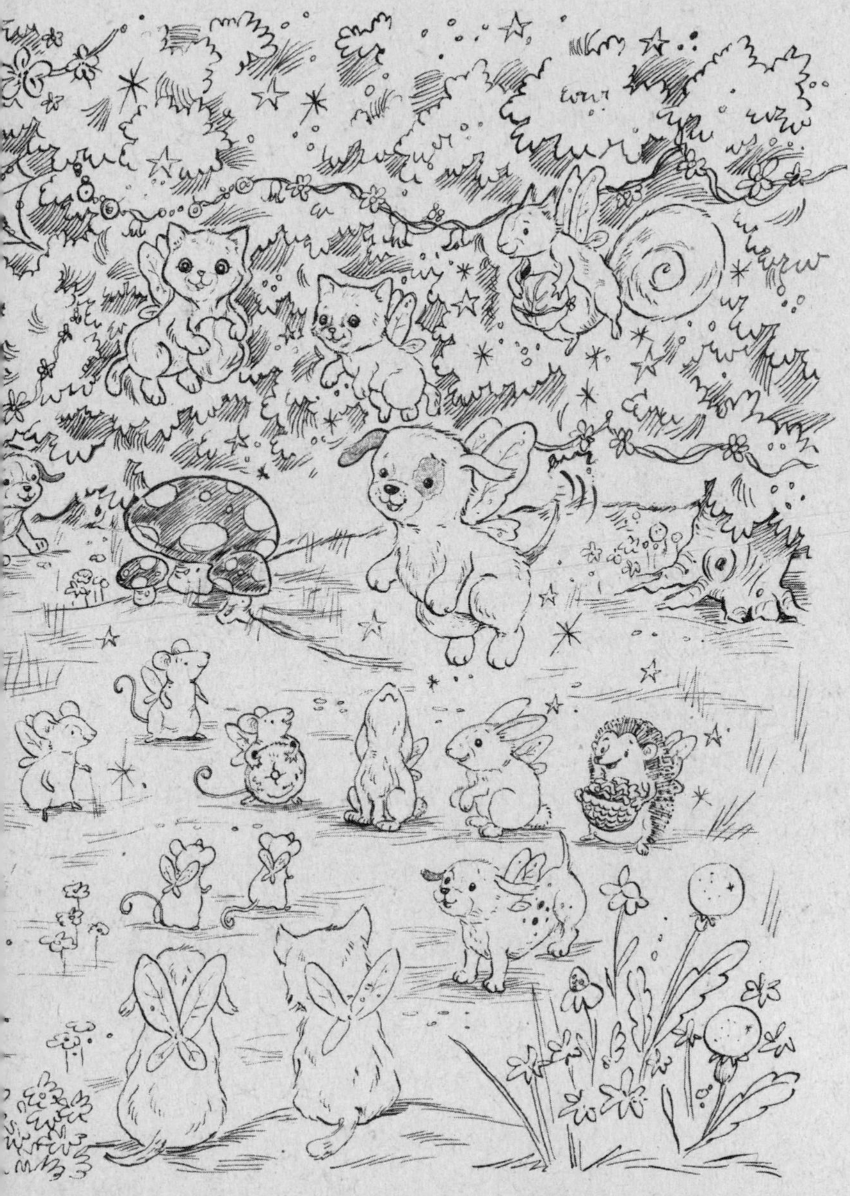

dream—only it was even prettier! The cobwebs shimmered with extra dewdrops, while garlands of bluebells and poppies adorned all the bushes.

The air filled with the sound of fluttering fairy wings as Paddy's friends came forward with presents. Even his new friends had brought gifts! Hattie had brought a bowl made of sycamore leaves. Magnifico had brought a miniature

moss cushion. And as for Sammy—first he filled the glade with shimmering stardust. Then, from behind his back, he brought out a whole parcel of conkers and acorns to play with!

"Time for games, everyone!" cried Paddy's dad.

Soon everyone had joined hands and they all danced in a circle, singing *Ring Around an Acorn* at the tops of their voices. Then

they played *Conker Catch*, before

spreading out to play *Hide the Acorn*.

Paddy had never had so much fun!

At last, happy and weary, they

gathered for the birthday picnic.

Paddy's mom had spread out a

big mat made of pearly reeds from

Moonshine Pond, and it was laden

with treats and delicacies. Paddy's
eyes nearly popped out when he
saw everything! There were cowslip
tarts, daisy pies, fairy fancies,
and buttercup buns, along
with more honeysuckle fizz and
elderflower juice than even Paddy
could dream of.

But before they began to dig in, Paddy's dad came bounding out of their den with something else. Paddy's tail began to wag.

Would it be . . . ?

Could it be . . . ?

Paddy yelped happily as his dad handed him a gift wrapped in silvery leaves. As Paddy began to pull at it with his teeth, he was so excited that his whole body started to tremble.

Would it be . . . ?

Could it be . . . ?

One corner of the wrapping came open. Paddy sniffed with his pink button nose.

It *smelled* like a bone.

He tore some more of the leaves away.

It *looked* like a bone.

The last piece of wrapping dropped off, and Paddy bounced up and down with joy.

It WAS a bone!

And it was even juicier and
tastier than the one he had seen in
his dream.

"Thank you, thank you!"

Paddy barked, jumping around in circles.

Everyone clapped and cheered, then they began to eat and drink. Paddy gave his bone one lick, then decided to save it for later. There was so much delicious party food, he wanted to try it all. As he slurped honeysuckle fizz and chomped a daisy pie, he decided that this really was the best birthday party ever!

113

In the distance, the sun was dipping toward Sundown Hill. Golden rays played with the stardust in the air, while the shadows in the clearing grew longer.

Paddy thought there couldn't possibly be any more treats. He'd had so many! But his mom and dad had disappeared again, and all the fairy guests began to whisper behind their paws. Where had Paddy's parents gone? What were they up to?

Suddenly, there was a flurry of fur at the entrance to the family den. Paddy turned to look and saw his mom, dad, and Pippa holding a birthday cake between them. It was made of hazelnuts and rosehips, and it had a garland of ivy leaves tied in a bow around it. On the top, waving gently, were birthday dandelion clocks for Paddy to blow.

Everyone cheered again, and burst into song.

"Happy birthday, dear Paddy! Happy birthday to you!" they chorused.

"Happy birthday, dear Paddy! Happy birthday to meeeee!" Paddy sang along. His tail was wagging so fast, it nearly blew all the seeds from the dandelion clocks!

Just as the song came to an end, Paddy heard something else. Something tuneful and tinkly. It was coming from their den. . . .

*Cheep!*

*Cheep cheep!*

*Cheep cheep cheep!*

Paddy cocked his ears. "What is that?" he asked.

His mom smiled. "It's the bluebird chicks!" she told him. "They've just hatched. There are three of them—come and look!"

With a last burst of energy, Paddy bounded over to the nest. And there they were—three tiny

balls of fluff, each with a teeny
beak, begging for food. And
to think they'd hatched on his
birthday. . . .

"They're the best present of
*all*!" Paddy cried.

"Well, we're all happy that
you've had such a lovely day." His
mom smiled. "But don't forget to
blow your birthday clocks!"

The birthday cake was sitting
in the middle of the picnic. Paddy

rushed back. As he filled his cheeks with air, he thought he was the luckiest Pollen Puppy in the whole of Misty Wood.

"One, two, three, *blow*!" chanted the crowd.

Paddy blew. The dandelion seeds flew up in a cloud, then floated off. Some of the guests laughed and chased after them.

But not Paddy. Paddy had finally run out of puff.

He lay down on his soft, mossy cushion and, with a happy sigh, he fell fast asleep.

# Misty Wood Word Search

Can you find all these words from
the story in this fun word search?

ACORN      GAME      TAIL
BONE       PARTY    WAG
DREAM     PRESENT
FLICK      PUPPY

```
E  A  C  O  R  N  O  E  O  H  S
B  E  H  V  S  G  A  M  E  N  N
O  P  F  H  N  I  E  H  P  S  R
N  E  D  I  S  T  T  A  R  R  E
E  P  I  S  O  H  H  E  E  S  I
D  R  W  A  G  Y  L  Y  S  T  T
R  L  A  H  T  P  I  C  E  S  E
E  U  E  R  S  F  M  I  N  A  D
A  U  A  S  Y  C  L  S  T  A  E
M  P  I  P  R  P  E  I  R  I  T
S  O  M  E  N  S  U  P  C  R  A
I  Y  O  R  W  G  R  P  A  K  I
F  E  M  H  L  I  H  F  P  R  L
N  R  T  P  A  C  E  E  V  Y  O
```

# All about YOUR Birthday!

When is your birthday?

_____

_____

How old will you be on your
next birthday?

_____

_____

What present would you like?

_____

_____

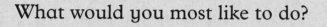

What would you most like to do?

_____

_____

Which people would you like to be there?

_____

_____

# A Very Happy Birthday!

Paddy gets VERY excited about his birthday. What are your three favorite things about birthdays?

1. _____

2. _____

3. _____

What other special occasions are really exciting?

1. _____

2. _____

3. _____

# Connect the Dots

Follow the numbers and connect all the dots to make a lovely picture. Start with dot number 1.

Can you guess what Paddy is holding?

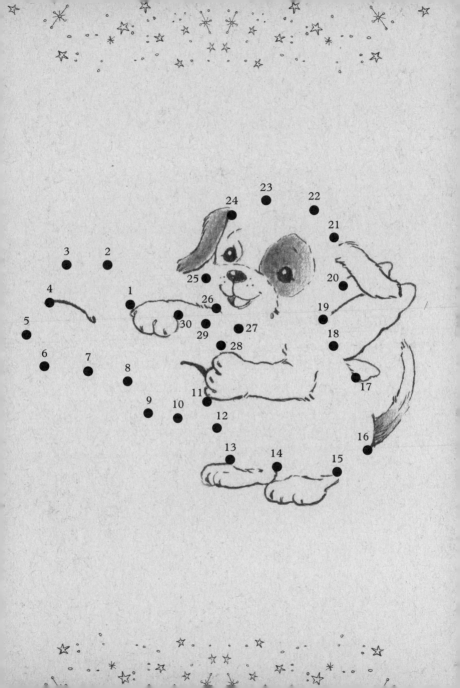

# Make Paddy a Birthday Card!

Can you design a special birthday card for Paddy?

Use the frame on the next page. Make the card as colorful as you can!

What kind of picture do you think Paddy would like on the front of his card?

Don't forget to write Paddy a nice message!